THE BOOK DOCTOR

THE BOOK DOCTOR

by

JOHN SCHERBER

SAN MIGUEL ALLENDE BOOKS

San Miguel de Allende Books
San Miguel de Allende, Guanajuato, Mexico

ACKNOWLEDGMENTS

Any book starts as an idea, and by its completion becomes a joint effort.

Thanks to my wife, Kristine, for editorial and critical help.Thanks to Marilyn Krichman for editorial and proofreading assistance.

Thanks to Jordyn Redwood for research assistance. Thanks to The Rosewood Hotel, San Miguel de Allende, GTO, México for their cooperation.

Cover photo: The Rosewood Hotel, San Miguel de Allende, by Lander Rodriguez.

Cover Design by Lander Rodriguez

Web Page Design by Julio Mendez

ISBN 978-0-9832582-6-1

San Miguel Allende Books
San Miguel de Allende, GTO, México
www.sanmiguelallendebooks.com

Also by John Scherber

NONFICTION
San Miguel de Allende: A Place in the Heart
A Writer's Notebook
Into the Heart of México
Living in San Miguel

FICTION
(The Murder in México series)
Twenty Centavos
The Fifth Codex
Brushwork
Daddy's Girl
Strike Zone
Vanishing Act
Jack and Jill
Identity Crisis
The Theft of the Virgin
The Predator
The Girl from Veracruz
Angel Face
Uneasy Rider
Lost in Chiapas

For Kristine

No writer wants to hear this, but it's the quality of the promotion more than the quality of the book that makes a best seller. Ask anyone in New York.

–Derek Hamilton

For writers it is always said that the first twenty years of life contain the whole of experience—the rest is observation.

–Graham Greene

CHAPTER ONE

Her name is Dr. Ruth," said my partner, Maya Sanchez, assembling a shrimp taco with an expertise born of long experience. We were sitting down to lunch in our San Miguel, México garden across from the thirty-foot bamboo towering over the east wall, where it got the full benefit of the afternoon sun. She had dressed the cast-iron table with an embroidered cotton cloth similar to the white peasant top she was wearing. The January sun was blazing, but we were shaded by a broad canvas umbrella large enough to cover the chairs as well as the tabletop.

"But I don't think we need her help, do we?" I said, surprised. I searched Maya's face for a moment. We'd been together eight years, but I hadn't noticed things slowing down. At thirty, she was hotter than ever. I always thought our relationship was the inspired connection between an artist from Ohio and a México City woman with a master's degree in history. The electricity was still crackling, and we shared a mental life that kept both of us balanced. "I thought we were doing OK in the bedroom. You would've said something about it otherwise." Not only was her English nuanced and flexible, but her mastery of American slang grew every day—she could have found the words to let me know quickly enough if we ever had a problem. Not that I wouldn't know it myself.

"We are doing OK, Paul, but she's not that kind of Dr. Ruth. Her last name is Bendickson, and she's a mystery writer. I told you about her last year when I was reading her books." As the Zacher Agency had grown more experienced over the last couple of years, Maya had gotten into mysteries, and I suspected she occasionally thought of writing one herself based on our cases, although she'd never brought it up to me directly. Knowing her mental process, I didn't expect to hear any detail about it until she had most of it worked out.

"That Ruth? I didn't know she was a doctor, too. Why is she still working after publishing those mysteries? She must've made a bundle." I don't read any mysteries, but I remembered that Maya had mentioned the incredible success of Ruth Bendickson. She'd come from nowhere to publish two blockbusters in quick succession, followed, after an interval, by a third book in the same series that was not quite up to the first two. Critics wrote that Ruth had strayed off course, which Maya said was not unusual after an initial success. Still, the third book was another bestseller because her fan base was huge and loyal.

"It's not that kind of doctor, she's got a Ph.D. in English. She teaches creative writing at Bolton College."

"Very prestigious," I said. "I read somewhere that they've resisted the pressure to become co-ed."

"What's that?"

"They still only admit women." Obviously, *co-ed* hadn't yet entered Maya's vernacular lexicon.

"Sounds like you could focus on your studies better without men around. I know I could."

"I think that's the idea. Of course, they don't have a football team." Maya thought by football I meant soccer, which is called *futbol* here.

"Anyway, I brought up her name again because she's the featured speaker at the International Mystery Writers' Conference this year." She squeezed a dollop of hot sauce onto her taco. She preferred the lethal *habanero*, the hottest Méxican variety, which to me tasted almost radioactive. I always settled for *serrano*, a mere single step up from *jalapeño*.

"And it's being held here in March. I saw that in *Atención*. So you'd like to meet her, or at least hear her presentation?"

"Sure, let's put it on the calendar," she said.

"But I have to tell you that I'm not certain writers like Ruth Bendickson know what really goes on in the lives of detectives in the trenches. I say that because we didn't know anything, either, when we started, and I assume she's never worked as one. Cody was a detective when we started, but you and I had to learn it by doing it. A writer would have to make up the detail, or research it by tagging along for a while, and if she's an academic, well…how close would she ever get to it?"

"Maybe she could consult with us while she's here. Why not? We know a lot more about it now, and we don't have any cases going."

"Consult with The Paul Zacher Agency? We're the underpaid grunts of the investigative world."

"Don't we get enough glory for you? *Pobrecito*! Poor baby!" She took my hand in consolation.

"Glory would be great, but usually I'll settle

for survival and getting paid. I can have glory on my tombstone, too. I don't mind waiting for it."

Some might think I was a little flip about this, but when we finished our ninth case with all of us still standing, I looked back on a string of tense moments where our survival had been in doubt too often. Sometimes we'd only managed by good fortune, a disturbing kind of support that could collapse at any time, like rickety scaffolding erected on spongy ground. Never available on call, you couldn't anticipate when luck was about to desert you. Maya had left me for three months about halfway through those cases because she couldn't control the risk around us, and she'd agreed to return only as head of the agency. Part of my acquiescence was that she came back to me personally as well. I continued as a staff investigator, although the agency retained my name as a nostalgic gesture to a less troubled time.

Cody Williams, our six-foot-three, 230-pound retired homicide detective from Illinois, was our procedural maven. When none of us knew what to do next, he could fake it better than either Maya or I could. He knew how to pick the locks, and possessed the mass to knock down the doors when his picks failed, or when we were in a hurry. He also knew what questions to ask. There were times when that was all we had, and in my heart, I knew we were probably no different from many other detective agencies in that way. Our current ace-in-the-hole card was one Cody had also brought us, his new girlfriend, Sheila Roper. She was a part-time psychic with an uncertain trajectory, so she was a natural fit. One reason I felt good about her was that she had brought it home for us on our last case, where the Virgin of Guadalupe was stolen when it was on tour across México. Of course, feeling good is not the same as trust. Trust is an edifice built on history, and we hadn't known her that long. At this point I was still never certain when Sheila said something whether it was her feelings or her gift speaking. I'm not sure that she knew either. There's an element of serendipity about the detective business that we don't mention in our brochure.

After lunch, since I'd never heard of it except in our newspaper, *Atención*, I looked up the International Mystery Writers Conference on the Internet. It was a big deal, if you believed the hype on their website, and every March it pitched its tent in a different warm-weather venue. I could see how it would be a great draw for writer wannabes suffering in cold climates, deadly sick of winter and eager to hang out with the published literati. Last year they'd convened in Orlando, two years ago in Scottsdale, and the year before that, they'd come to earth in some palmy resort outside of San Jose, Costa Rica, nearer the beach. They billed themselves as bilingual and multicultural. To me, it sounded like the conference had touched all the right bases. I understood why they'd chosen to come to San Miguel this year. Here, 10,000 expatriates rub shoulders with 65,000 locals. Writers and painters are disproportionately represented, even if most of them didn't write or paint that much. After all, México is a laid-back kind of place and people here tend to accept without question what you call yourself.

Of course, at 6400 feet up on a mountain plateau, we're not a beach community. You'd have to dress indecently to get sunburned in March, but afternoon highs consistently reach the 80s with low humidity, and the angular sun does its eager part almost every day. If you were coming from Manchester, Vermont; Billings, Montana; or Calgary, it makes sense in a compelling way. It probably didn't matter if you could write, simply hanging out at the conference with people who did made it worthwhile. For the conference fee, plus hotel, airfare, and meals, you could feel like a winner in print, although the conference website said they gave you a bag lunch. As Maya had mentioned, this year the renowned Ruth Bendickson would be among us as the featured speaker, her slightest gesture launching fairy dust in clouds over the wannabe literati.

The event also touted lesser stars in mid-rank positions. One was Bill Masterson, who wrote wildly popular mysteries that were dressed up as travel books. Each one was set in a different exotic locale. His blurb made it sound like his detective could knock back a lot of rum or tequila while half-dressed women dropped to their knees at his approach. This would be a specialty following; some would call it a niche, but I suspected it was not small. Whether Masterson was the real deal, or only offered some fantasy on the beach, I didn't plan to investigate.

Another mentor was Justus Barlow, a name I also didn't know. His blurb explained that he was a book doctor, one who had assisted at the birth of nearly two dozen best selling novels. The slogan, *beating them into condition*, was used to describe his preferred technique. Was it authors or their manuscripts taking the blows? It sounded kinky to me. I didn't know any writers, other than Maya, but if they're like painters, I could understand the phrase. Barlow offered to have meetings with potential clients during the conference, based on a pre-submitted sample, all for an extra fee, not disclosed on the website. If you recovered from the initial assault, you could apply to be his student. I suppose it was determined by the condition of the manuscript in question. As a painter, I knew that making progress in the arts often requires some degree of suffering, but I had never seen it spelled out so forthrightly. Two or three additional featured speakers of lower rank were listed, plus numerous breakout sessions, an hour or so long, where all kinds of subjects were treated in a more cursory fashion by experts whose credentials were not disclosed in detail. Maybe they were friends of the director. If I sound cynical, it's because, as a painter, I don't believe in the effectiveness of this kind of group hug.

It was at this point, near the bottom of the webpage, that I noticed that admission to the conference was $495. Had we been working a paid case at the moment, I might have justified it, but as an amusement, I didn't think it had merit, at least, not for Cody and me. Maya did, however, and she's head of the agency.

"I think we should go," she said, "why not?"

"Cody and I aren't capable of writing so much as a grocery list. Your case is naturally somewhat different, now that you're published, but you're not writing any mysteries." Maya's book on the early years of our town's revolutionary hero, Ignacio

Allende, had been out and struggling to find an audience for almost two years.

"But you always write the case reports."

"Yes, but I'm working from our notes, and we would never show them to anyone, except at gunpoint. It's only to have a record for our own files. You should attend if you think you'll get something from it, but for Cody and me, it would be a waste of time and money. If you go, you can tell Ruth Bendickson in person how much you like her books. Cody and I will stay behind to solve cases and make money." We both knew we didn't have anything on the horizon. I was also struggling to find a new painting idea, so it was like being in a mental vacuum. I tried to think of these periods as restful, but they felt more like frustration.

But then, two days later, we got involved in an urgent missing person case that turned out to be a couple's dust up that paid nothing, and while we were sorting it out, Maya didn't follow up on the conference for two weeks. When the subject came up again, I thought she'd forgotten about it, because I had. Then, when she was just about to enroll, we received an email from the director, a person named Chad Metcalf, asking if we would like to be participants in the conference and give what he called "a breakout session on the activities and pro-cedures of a genuine working detective agency." Of course, we were the only such organization in San Miguel, and Metcalf must have known that. Maya suggested that our credibility had been en-hanced because she was, after all, a published author.

"What does it pay?" I asked. Since Maya wrote the checks for the bills, this was normally her question.

"They're offering attendance at the confer-ence for all three of us, and the chance to promote our business to people attending. They're expecting almost two hundred this year. I also get to sell my book in their bookstore."

I called Cody and signed him up. He grumbled a bit about missing a football game or two, but that was no different when we had an active case. Any-way, by the time the conference started early in March, the Super Bowl was only a drunken memory for most.

CHAPTER TWO
THE BOOK DOCTOR IS IN

Justus Barlow sat next to the weathered sill of the single sliding window in his drab hotel room in the Méxican hill town of San Miguel de Allende. As he watched, outside in the courtyard three dark-haired children under ten years of age played at the concrete edge of a long, narrow swimming pool. No lifeguard was present. In México, if they drowned, it would mean they were fated to drown since birth. Ten muscular lifeguards sitting at poolside under beach umbrellas couldn't have saved them. But Justus Barlow didn't know this. He thought their parents were negligent, just as the conference had been negligent in failing to book him a better room at their own expense. In his own mind, Justus Barlow was a person of consequence.

The other wings of the two-story hotel, covered in plum-colored stucco, bracketed the courtyard. All the windows were framed in aluminum. The construction details suggested 1970, a bad year for hotel architecture anywhere. Now the building felt dated and bland. The upkeep had suffered. Had it looked like 1700, which was how the central part of San Miguel looked, it would have suited Justus Barlow much better, because he had some taste, but then his room would have cost much more than the $36 a night the conference was paying. He gave a long sigh and bit into an apple before setting it down on the tattered title page of a manuscript, where, as he chewed, it rested at the intersection of two brown coffee cup rings. He returned to the present with a start and looked again at the woman sitting across the room from him.

"And another thing," he said, swallowing, "is that the personality of Carrie is not merely flawed, it's dead wrong. It falls flat. What kind of name is that for a character? It's a better fit for a beast of burden." He nearly chuckled at the implicit pun as his right arm made a broad gesture of dismissal. "Carrie would work much better if, instead of trying to be cutting edge and writing a graphic novel, she were inspired by Jane Austen."

This had popped into Barlow's head from nowhere, and he held up an index finger to emphasize the point. "Because Carrie herself *is* like a Jane Austen character, or she should be, if she hadn't been written by the seat of your pants with no thought as to how she would function in the plot. *That* should be the central irony of your book. And irony is something you overlook at your peril, Lisa. A fictionalized account of your life as a writer is not remarkable or compelling in itself, but imagine the interest if you'd been misplaced in time! Then you'd have some real *tension*; can you see that? Right now it's no more than limp. The vacancy of her character makes the whole book wilt around her. If you stood it on edge and leaned it against the wall, it would sag in the middle."

Justus Barlow enjoyed this image—it almost made him think he could write himself.

Lisa Givens looked up at him from the spot she'd been staring at on the floor by her feet. It was the midpoint of a lightning crack that went from one corner diagonally to the other of a large ceramic tile. Since she'd met him in person for the first time in San Miguel, she'd found herself cringing when she talked to him. It had been easier before, when all their sessions had been by phone.

"But, Mr. Barlow, that's not the way I imagined Carrie. She could never be a Jane Austen character. She never even thinks about getting married. Carrie is driven by art, the art of writing. I saw her as woman as a creative person."

"Then call her Elizabeth or Catherine, for Christ's sake, something upstanding. Give her a name with substance and dignity. Carrie's no better than Tiffany or Amber. If you're going to be a writer, then start by getting serious about names—they cue your reader what to think from page one. Also, try to remember that you're not writing for people your own age—they don't read anymore. They're too busy texting."

"I think both those names are too old fashioned." She couldn't look Barlow in the face as she said this. He ignored her comment.

"I think Carrie is *forced* to work on a graphic novel, even though she *hates* it. She doesn't understand what it is. Her boyfriend is making her do it because he thinks that's where the money is. And he has no idea that she's really a person from the early nineteenth century. What she needs most is someone to help her lace up her corset, but she can't bring herself to say it." Barlow took another bite of the apple and looked back out the window. He didn't care for Lisa's body language, although she wasn't bad looking. Great writers never cringed. He tried to imagine

Tolstoy cringing, kneeling on the tail of his beard.

"No, she loves it, Mr. Barlow! That's what she lives for. No one is forcing her to do her book that way." Justus Barlow watched her pale eyebrows rise in indignation. They were as vague and undefined as her character.

"Have you listened to anything at all that I've been telling you about dramatic tension? Why do you think you're paying me $85 an hour? It's because I *know* about this stuff, OK? I've made nineteen books into best sellers, and some of them were no better than this...frail piece of pulp, when they came to me." If the apple core hadn't been resting on the manuscript, he would have picked the document up and waved it at her, but he didn't want to set the core's sticky bottom on the desktop.

Lisa's shoulders sagged further. "I only thought that..."

"And this Clint, Chet, or Chuck, whatever his name is. Why is he such a pathetic pussy? He's supposed to be a boxer, isn't he? He ought to be able to take a hit or two."

"I was trying to play him against type. He's sensitive to Carrie's needs. Isn't that what you've been suggesting? He can do that because he's a real man. Anyway, his name is Chick."

"Chick! Chick? You see what I mean? Jesus, so why does he have a girl's name? You're trying to sell me a boxer named Chick? Give me a break here! He'd be carried out of the ring on a stretcher every night. It would be a point of honor for every opponent to level him in the first round."

"But I don't ever show him in a match. That's all backstory. He retired at twenty-eight, and now he owns a bookstore. That was always his dream. He was only boxing to get the capital for inventory."

Barlow gave her a fishy look, one he saved for his greenest clients. "So don't give me flashbacks either. Nothing stops a story dead in its tracks like a flashback. Did you even spend a single moment researching boxing?"

"I didn't need to. This book is not about boxing. Chick plans to use his publishing industry connections to get Carrie's book published."

"Read some Hemingway, then, do some investigation. Make it real! Show this Chick fellow taking a stout blow or two to the face. It's potentially disfiguring. His mouth is distorted on impact. His lip splits, his teeth are loose, and his broken nose dribbles blood over his chin. The male reader will connect with that. I don't think you're getting this, girl, and now I'm worried that you never will. You've got a boxer who's a character, and I'll bet you've never been to a single match in your life." Barlow leaned back in his chair and, with a series of careful, precise bites, as if extracting the last nickel of value from the apple, finished it and dropped the core back on the manuscript, where it bounced once and rolled over, leaving a row of parallel moist dots like a trail of tears.

Lisa said nothing more for three or four minutes, looking helplessly at her hands, which didn't move. Barlow thought the skin looked rough, and the fingers stubby, neither of which he excused easily. She was, he thought, a charmless person, although she had a good body—not that it would last. Lisa reminded him of another equally helpless client, one from more than five years back, a woman named Amy Wendt, who had never fulfilled her promise. Where was this Lisa's finesse? Had she no insight? Did he have to do everything for these people? So it seemed in this business, but they would damn well pay for it. Barlow's level of expertise never came cheaply. He leaned back in his chair and closed his eyes as an insight came to him. It was followed by a serious look. His brow collected in a row of vertical creases like exclamation points.

"Now that I'm here, and you are too, for the conference, I think we're going to need many more sessions than I originally planned; like every day, going forward from this point. It's a perfect opportunity to hash this out face-to-face, one we might never have again. This is it, OK? You live in Denver, right, and I live in the Village, that's been the problem up until now."

"Laramie."

His hand clawed the vagueness of the air between them. "Whatever. It's all the same out there. I came down to San Miguel early for some dental work, which is much cheaper here than on the East Coast, so why not just pick me up after each session, all those root canals—you *are* renting a car?—and then we can come back here and get this feeble monster ready for New York." In a more upbeat frame of mind, thinking now that he might be able to pay his dental bills after all, Barlow reached over to seize her hand, but it remained rigidly in her lap. He slapped his knee instead, as if that was his original intention.

"Now I am *so* excited," he said, expansively, "we've got such a good deal going. For you, I mean. Wow! For me, it's always about the client. I'm here for you. Wanna stay for a glass of wine, Lisa? I won't charge you for it, even though it's what I drink myself."

Glancing at his watch, Justus Barlow leaned

over and made another entry in a long column of numbers in his spiral notebook as Lisa got to her feet and disappeared into the bathroom.

CHAPTER THREE

A college friend of mine, now a stockbroker, arriving in San Miguel for a visit from a bright, upscale enclave of Los Angeles, said that, on first impression, this town reminded him of Beirut, which he knew only from television journalism. Although we lack both a Hezbollah chapter and a falafel stand here, he still ranted at length about our crumbling buildings and their rotting masonry. He found offensive the puckering stucco that sometimes drops in sheets onto the stone pavements. He said the ancient church cupolas festooned with pigeon droppings grossed him out. In passing, he had once looked into the unshuttered street-side window of a centuries old home on Aldama, and saw the roof collapsed upon the rubble within. A fixer-upper, perhaps, I replied calmly, but here, never a ruin. It was as if he didn't hear me. Painting has taught me that you can put different scenes in front of people, but you will not change their point of view.

"But wait," I added, "You'll find no shell holes in this town! It's not Syria!" I stopped short of saying that they'd all been filled in since the last revolution. Yes, this place has a weathered, lived-in look, but it was founded in 1542. You've got to expect layers of patina. When I look at it, I see the mellow amber and ocher shades of the old stucco walls, the deep shadows in the contours of carved stonework, the battered public fountains that still produce refreshment for street burros and country horses so they can sustain the heat of the day. This has not changed since our own *insurgente*, Ignacio Allende, heroically led his native troops off to defeat by their Spanish colonial masters in 1810. Brave as it is, heroism in México has often been only a flash in the pan, but nonetheless, one with inspiring reverberation throughout history. The problem has usually been that the ammunition ran out long before the courage failed.

Now, within these historic, battered walls, the cool, sheltered gardens whisper of afternoon repose. In my mind, the black-haired and dark-eyed *señoritas* still move about in long dresses beneath the stone arches. Sensing your appreciative gaze, they turn to smile back at you over their bare shoulders.

Yet, although it may sound like it, I'm not sentimental about San Miguel. It has its warts, and it's not for every gringo who may yearn to bolt from Escanaba in February. It would never, for example, be a suitable location for the driven, type-A personality, nor for the perfectionist of any stripe. Neither is it suitable for the person who is fond of saying, "Only the best is good enough for me." This town is usually not the best, nor is it the most perfect, nor is it going anywhere in a big hurry, but it's still a pretty damn good place to live. And that's good enough for me and my own dark-eyed *señorita*, Maya Sanchez.

So I was not distressed when some big money (you would never know exactly where it originated, although I have heard it was from Colorado) came into San Miguel and put up a hotel on the back lot of the ancient Canal family hacienda on the Ancha de San Antonio, where the two-block-long surviving building at the front is currently the Instituto Allende. It now specializes in weekend craft fairs and lavish weddings for the elites of México City in search of character and charm for the nuptials of their pampered offspring. I refer to these affairs as *mariachi* weekends.

This old hacienda is a deep property with an agricultural history. The new hotel development is bordered by a series of townhouses, which, like the principal building, are all in the neo-colonial style. With proper colors and the carved *cantera* stonework, it's all authentically done, and reminds me of what a great colonial property might have looked like if they had ever wanted to build one four stories high. Of course, they never thought of it here. Even three was a skyscraper. Back then, four may have been seen as trying to get too close to heaven without deserving it, and thus tempting the unavoidable backlash of fate.

I hadn't spent much time at this new Rosewood Hotel. I'd never eaten at their high-end restaurant on the main floor, called *1826*, but twice Maya and I had come for sunset drinks at the rooftop bar, usually when we'd just been settled out on a case. Twice more Cody and Sheila came with us. Nonetheless, I understood why this was the venue chosen by the International Mystery Writers' Conference for their San Miguel meeting. When before I had pictured them in a tent, I was selling them short. There must be some money in these affairs. If they even brought in only 150 people, it would be close to $75,000 just for the basic admission. Naturally, from looking at the brochure, I knew there were many potential add-ons.

Their choice of venue encouraged the attendees to conclude the conference was a classy operation. I had no reason to think it wasn't; I knew nothing about it, except that the director wanted the presence of the Paul Zacher Agency for an hour and twenty minutes, including questions from the audience. We were all excited as we walked through the *porte cochere* and into the hotel lobby that first morning. The crowd around us was excited too as we lined up at the reception desk on the lower level to collect our identification badges. The lines were divided between Faculty and Conference Attendees. At the far end, another, much smaller sign read, Single Ticket Holders. Were these people who couldn't come up with $495 and settled for smaller portions? We were cleared at the Faculty line without incident and issued laminated badges dangling on ropey cords. Walking down the adjacent corridor under stone arches, we were unsure what would happen next. We studied the programs in our hands, facing the first of a series of choices we'd never had to make before. I felt out of my element and I knew Cody did too, but Maya was excited.

Only a writers' conference would begin by offering a presentation by Justus Barlow entitled, *The Death of the Adverb*. I was speculating there, but really, the eyes roll back in anticipation. Only as the first item of the day's business could such a talk draw an excited crowd ready to listen, and only then because their minds were empty and aching for recuperative structure after the previous night's opening fiesta. The margarita residues must have been still sloshing in their heads like waves on a remote and deserted shore. Of course, fiestas are nothing new to people who live here, so we hadn't attended. Our own homegrown fiestas are the best. This morning, Maya had chosen to take in an alternate session on book promotion, which she had been indignant to discover much earlier was entirely up to her, once she'd been published. For Cody and me, even the Justus Barlow talk on adverbs looked more interesting than Maya's choice of a presentation called, *Social Networking Interaction—Tweet Your Reader and She'll Retweet You!* This sounded slightly naughty, or possibly even illegal in México, although the country has gradually loosened up in recent years.

To me, Twitter is something the birds noisily practice within the bamboo on our east wall. I mainly wanted to catch the flavor of these early conference meetings so we could decide how much time we wanted to spend on the ones we weren't giving ourselves. I suspected it wouldn't be much, but you could never decide without a sample or two. Our own talk was scheduled for the first hour of the following day.

Cody and I took our seats near the back of a medium-sized conference room. Overhead I saw a provision to divide it in half if needed. At the front wall a slot in the ceiling held a rolled up projection screen. A man who must have been Chad Metcalf, the director, had already begun the introduction.

"… now conclude by saying that he is not only one of the great incubators of literary talent in the United States, but also a great personal friend of mine, Mr. Justus Barlow!"

Nodding to the crowd, Barlow waited for the applause to die before approaching the platform. His gait was awkward. With one leg evidently shorter than the other, each stride looked like he was pausing to step on something noxious. The shorter leg was buttressed by a thicker heel and sole on that shoe, but it still gave him a curious side-to-side swagger as he mounted the two steps to the podium. Shoulder pads inflated his pinstriped jacket and provided a broader base for his slightly oversize head. Barlow looked to be about fifty years old and noticeably shorter than average, about five-foot-six. His straight black hair showed no sign of gray. Taking a moment to arrange his notes next to his water glass, he peered through thick lenses at the audience as if into a cave perpetually darkened by ignorance. Then he paused and cleared his throat away from the mike, behind his fist.

"Dearly beloved of this seventh annual mystery writers' conference! With no regret, I've come before you today to announce the passing of the English language adverb. It was summoned away unlamented and unmourned—nor will it be missed by real writers. No friends were present at the end, because there were none. It was buried in an unmarked grave in a potter's field. Any functions it once had have now been assumed by its muscular uncle, the verb—an insignificant addition to his task list."

Barlow paused for a moment, but no one rose to challenge this. Looking around, I had the sense that most people in the audience were still digesting it. He allowed an ironic smile to linger on his lips for an instant, as if to say, "Now I've got them eating out of the palm of my hand." Cody nudged me in the ribs and raised his eyebrows; a way of asking what this was about. As Barlow resumed, I couldn't have told him.

"You may ask: whatever did the late adverb achieve in its lengthy and tedious life? I can tell you this: nothing that was not better accomplished by the correct verb. The adverb stood to reinforce weak verb choices that would never have been made by a skilled writer. It allowed mere scribblers to pretend to describe action in terms that were pale and inadequate, bolstered by adverbial props. It helped a pink verb pretend to be scarlet, the taupe to be chestnut, and the gray verb to act is if its heart were black. It required us to believe that hesitant was forceful. We were never fooled! (Someone clapped a single time, as if she had slapped a mosquito.)

In life, the late adverb was never more than a shallow pretense, a transparent bluff on the stage of language, always in a distant supporting role. At curtain call, it never appeared with the rest of the cast to take a bow. In a film, it would've been called a mere *extra*." The echo of Barlow's voice died away before his next sentence. "What an apt description that would be, my friends, an *extra*." Barlow spit the last word into the gathering with visible contempt, as if he didn't care where it landed. Pausing to look at his notes, his face darkened, and a knot of veins puckered his forehead. He sensed their presence and tried to brush them away. A woman near the rear raised a tentative hand, and he waved her question away.

"So, what is our mission in this new, streamlined era? How can we emerge and go forward without this verbal fig leaf? It was never adequate to its self-assigned... its self-self assigned t-t-task."

Blinking several times, Barlow took a long breath and shook his head as if to clear it. The crowd waited in anticipation. I was now getting more interested myself, not so much in the content, but from the physical drama that was beginning to play out on the podium. Barlow looked disturbed, and it was not as if he'd forgotten what came next. I sensed he had given this talk before, and more than once.

With a tense grimace, he suddenly gripped both sides of the podium as if to lift it from the platform and hurtle it into the crowd. His body swayed from side to side, and with a look of shock on his face that gradually slackened into dismay, his knees buckled and he fell over backwards. The podium landed on top of him. His water glass emptied over the platform, rolled to one side, and shattered when it hit the limestone floor below. Justus Barlow did not struggle to get up: he did not move at all.

Leaping to its feet, yet still holding back in shock, the crowd leaned toward the platform even as it froze in silence. Chad Metcalf's silver head bobbed along the opposite aisle as he raced toward the front. Cody and I sprinted along the wall from the left. Rounding the front corner at the same time as we did, Metcalf had his cell out. He was punching on it as he arrived at Barlow's side ahead of us.

We held back along the front row, waiting to lend a hand if needed. I assumed Metcalf was calling an ambulance, but when he hung up he made no other move. Cody lunged for the platform and lifted the podium off Barlow's body, standing it on the corner out of the way. Blood covered the speaker's lips, and it appeared that the leading edge of the slanted surface had broken off one or more of his teeth as he'd pulled it down onto himself. The crowd began to murmur more loudly. People eagerly pressed forward. I heard a crunch as if someone had stepped on Barlow's glasses, which must have flown over the side when he went down. Cody rose to face the crowd, and with his arms extended in an authoritative, almost Papal, position, forced everyone backward into the room.

To me, Barlow looked finished, wiped out. His eyes stared at the ceiling without focus or movement, and an unnatural slackness had wilted his features, one that I had seen before; it was the final relaxation of death. Addressing the crowd, he had seemed animated and high strung. Now his cheeks sagged, and his mouth hung open half an inch. I could see that part of the blood on his face came from biting his tongue. I placed my fingers on his neck at various points, but found no pulse. My own heart was racing.

"The ambulance is now on the way," yelled Metcalf, over the buzzing of the crowd.

I didn't think it was going to help, but it wasn't my call. In his final moments Barlow had made no gestures of chest pain; he hadn't grabbed his left arm, which is common in a coronary. Before it slackened, his feverish grip on the podium was almost shaking. The agonized expression on his face—it seemed like he was gnashing his teeth—had resembled a seizure, even as he was overcome with a weakening dizziness that drove the tension from his body. Someone was going to have to start CPR. I wasn't eager, but I couldn't just let him go. I had a vague idea how to do it, although I'd never tried it before.

I knelt at Barlow's left side while I loosened his tie and opened the top two buttons of his shirt. When I unbuttoned his jacket and pulled it open I felt his keys in one pocket and his wallet in the other. He was still unresponsive, with his eyes open in my direction, but without seeing me, or anything at all. I forced his jaws open wider and located his two broken-off teeth along the left side of his tongue. I set them next to his head—what else could I do with them? His mouth was full of that flood of saliva, now tinted with blood, that suggested be might've been about to vomit when he went down.

"Do you know how to do this, Paul?" Cody asked. A moment later someone seized my shoulder, and I turned to see a man of about thirty dropping to his knees next to me.

"I'm a doctor," he said. "Let me do this. Thanks for clearing his airway." I yielded without protest as I stood up and stepped out of his way.

"Let's collect some names," Cody said from the edge of the platform. He must have assumed too that Barlow was gone, because he was now starting the investigation. With both hands elevated, waving at the crowd, he said more loudly. "Who was sitting in the front row just now when he fell? Please come forward."

I rinsed the blood and saliva off my hands with a bottle of water someone handed me, I didn't notice who, and Cody and I both pulled out our notebooks and started on opposite ends at the front of the crowd, gathering names and contact numbers of witnesses to talk with later if Barlow turned out to be the victim of a crime. After we both had about eight, Cody stepped up on the platform and asked everyone to leave the room so the medics could get to work when they arrived. Just as the last of the audience was departing, the ambulance crew rushed in and replaced the young doctor. They weren't on the platform five seconds before they resumed resuscitation.

I took a lingering look back at Barlow as we moved away at the rear of the crowd. With each chest compression, his body recoiled like a slab of meat. Who was this man? A pompous, self-important person who had thought it was within his purview to dispatch one of the seven parts of speech. I was startled by that. Was he powerful enough to change the English language singlehanded? If so, why wasn't he the keynote speaker? I didn't know much about it, but it seemed to me that only great writers could do that, and only because they had acquired an enormous following. I thought of Joyce or Hemingway; Faulkner—Maya would know better than I would. Maybe Barlow thought he was potentially of their stature, although nothing in the conference brochure indicated he was a writer. His physical problems must certainly have colored his view of the world— perhaps towering ambition compensated for his small frame. Other than that, I knew nothing about him. What Barlow was trying to do sounded to me like being told I could never use certain colors as a painter because I ran the risk of misusing them. I couldn't be trusted to use them properly. It was like being forced to cut off a finger because I might pick my nose with it, never mind all the legitimate uses for it. Had I been knowledgeable enough to stand up at the end of Barlow's address and ask a question, it would have been, "Why not talk about making strong verb choices instead? Why reduce people's choices? Why be a *limiter*? Where's the trust?"

Of course, to me, the controlling instinct revered by some people always lacked appeal. Maybe I didn't understand the master–student relationship. I'd never been a teacher—I'd always been on the student side of the desk, looking for the openness of guidance rather than the rigid confinement of ironclad rules. I walked away shaking my head.

Outside in the corridor, people milled about in shock. I went into the men's room and washed my hands, and then Cody and I filtered through the crowd toward the common area in order to move clear of the chaos. A staff person opened two sets of French doors at the lobby that gave onto the floor of an outdoor amphitheater with rows of seats rising up toward ground level.

"What do you think?" I asked, once we were outside. It was a brilliant March day, and it opened up above us like a shroud had been pulled away.

"I don't know. To me, what we saw didn't behave like a coronary. I've never witnessed anything like that. It wasn't a stroke either, the way he suddenly tensed up right before he went slack, because both his hands looked like they were working in the same way. Strokes happen on one side or the other, not both. It might have been a seizure of some kind, but not like one I've ever seen. Yet certainly it wasn't epileptic, either."

"Poison?" For some reason, I was still thinking it was murder. It was the first impression I had when Barlow went over on his back. "There's something symbolic about taking a man down in front of a crowd, especially when he's dispatching part of the language as if it were his sole decision to make. If it was murder it shows a lethal degree of contempt for him. Think of John Kennedy, taken out in front of the cheering masses. That's about power as well as assassination. It's much different from a knife in the back in a dark alley, which is only about death. Maybe Barlow was contemptuous of people he worked with too, and this was payback from one of his clients, a way of putting him down both figuratively and literally."

Cody gave me a somber look. "You really are thinking it was murder? Other than the impression it makes, this is an awfully public venue to kill someone in, so you'd better get it right if you try. And if it was poison, it wasn't instantaneous, so how can the poisoner predict where Barlow would be when it struck?"

"Maybe the killer didn't care, other than that Barlow die in public. Any place would be humiliating." Not knowing much about poison, I shrugged. My main argument in favor of the idea was that, in the absence of a coronary, a stroke, or an injury like a gunshot or being hit by a bus, people usually went into a decline before they died, particularly if they weren't that old. Most of us don't suddenly tense up, relax like a rubber band snapping, and drop to the floor at the age of fifty. On the other hand, Justus Barlow looked like he'd had a variety of lingering physical problems all his life. What finished him might have been gestating for a long time, perhaps since birth. Cody and I threaded our way through the agitated confusion that was now spilling out around us into the amphitheater. We walked up the steps toward the lobby and courtyard level.

There we ran into Licenciado Diego Delgado coming in. As one of the two principal investigators of the judicial police for San Miguel, he's been a fixture in almost all our cases. As usual, his medium brown suit looked like it was ready for a press. In tow he had Paco Mora, the medical examiner, and

Fernando Esquivel, his forensics man. Mora's normal practice was plastic surgery, serving the needs of distressed Americans whose mirrors no longer showed them the desired image. After the usual greetings, required even in a scene like that, Delgado took Cody and me by the elbow in a friendly, but nonetheless, authoritative, way.

"You will kindly be my guides through this crime, my good friends. I am sure you already have some excellent ideas."

"The ambulance crew called you?" Cody asked. "We weren't sure it was a crime."

"Yes, because they think they have not seen this cause of death before, and they have seen many more than I have. Who can say? It is worth a look, especially when you have a gathering of so many important gringos at the Rosewood Hotel."

We descended the limestone steps back down to the meeting room level.

"Did the medics speculate on what it might've been?" I said.

"They offered no opinion, but they wanted us to look at the scene before it was disturbed. Now I am so happy to have the two finest witnesses in San Miguel to tell me the real story. I assume you were there when it happened? Because you have a proven knack for landing in the vicinity of trouble."

"Because it follows us," I said. "We don't have to work at it."

"We didn't recognize the cause of death either," said Cody. "The victim's speech stumbled only a little, then he grew rigid for an instant before relaxing suddenly. He went over backwards as if his back had constricted and then abruptly released all its tension. He brought the lectern down on top of himself. We got to him first, and he was no longer breathing. A doctor from the crowd worked on him for a while before the ambulance got here."

"He was completely unresponsive," I said. "Not even a flutter. Here's a list of the people who were sitting in the front row when he went down." I peeled off that damp page of my notebook. Cody did the same.

Although Delgado was impressed by our diligence, we didn't have much more to tell him, and after a few minutes we left him to work the scene with his crew. By then, the ambulance people had already taken the body away. Here in México, the crew would never work on you for even half an hour, because that would oppose fate. The medics could get in serious trouble themselves with the powers that ran the universe by doing that. They knew their limits to the letter. To me, this looked like a case for the autopsy team in Guanajuato, the state capital. Until he received their report, Delgado wouldn't be moving forward on the case and we'd have the field to ourselves.

I figured if we wanted to speak with the front row witnesses later, we could get a copy of our lists from his office. At that point we didn't have a case, either, or any realistic prospect of getting one, but seeing someone murdered makes me want to get involved. I'd also seen how Cody had responded reflexively when Barlow went down. It's my meddling nature, something I hadn't discovered about myself until I got into this business. Maybe it was only what Maya called my Boy Scout instincts. They'd lured us into several cases where we had no client and no expectation of being paid or even thanked. It never gave us pause until we went to pay the bills at the end.

Cody and I walked back upstairs, where everything looked normal. Once we were out of earshot of the police and the conference group, now dispersing below, he said, "I know what you're thinking."

"Of course. We'll solve the murder. That's what detectives do." We went outside under the *porte cochere.* A family from México City, all wearing Polo, was watching as the staff unloaded luggage from their BMW 740i.

"Got any ideas on how we're going to do that?"

"I know how we're going to start." I reached into my pants pocket and pulled out Justus Barlow's room key, dangling it before Cody's nose. "I lifted it from his jacket pocket before I gave up the CPR to the doctor."

Cody nodded as if this were no surprise. "I'll give you ten out of ten for practical. Where was he staying?"

"At the Hacienda Old México. Delgado will establish that for himself with no problem once he decides to investigate, if he ever does. I figured that, having no standing in this case, we wouldn't be able to get into his room as easily as the police can, and they won't be on their way for some time. I want to look at that room the way Barlow left it, or with only a superficial cleaning."

"Not exactly a luxury facility. I don't mind being ahead of Delgado on this one. He'll be along eventually. Let's check it out."

From the Rosewood Hotel, we walked two blocks down Calle Nemesio Diez and then several blocks up the Ancha de San Antonio. Old fashioned was too polite a phrase to describe the Hacienda Old México, and we were no longer in a polite frame of mind. Surely it held no trace of faded gentility. We have a lot of old fashioned hostelries to stay in when visiting San Miguel, many of them charming beyond words, partly because they truly are old and don't need to work at being charming, but the Old México had simply been let go. It looked like a place Americans might have flocked to during the Nixon era. They would've felt like they were South of the Border, a term which then described a state of mind more than a real place. Maybe it still is, but you don't hear the phrase as much. Because the hotel was situated on a large property, and even had its own small bullring and parking lot, I thought its main value was as a potential redevelopment site, if the rabid American press ever stopped scaring the tourists away. The Canadians were still coming in large numbers, and they survived quite well. I didn't think it was because they were smarter or braver, only that they were lied to less in their home media.

Without pausing at the desk to ask for directions, we found Barlow's room on the second floor, overlooking the courtyard and the pool. The corridors still displayed the old cylindrical chrome floor-model ashtrays at the base of the stairwells. The sand, now the color of ash, had begged for replacement for some time. We knocked softy at Barlow's door before using the key, in case he had some adoring *señorita* awaiting his return, but that seemed doubtful. Once inside, we could have been in any cheap motel anywhere. It might have been Scotts Bluff or South St. Paul. I could see the book doctor waking up in the morning and pulling on his glasses to check his room receipt to remind himself where he was on the current leg of his adverb assassination tour. The only art in view was a faded paper print of Our Lady of Guadalupe in a black lacquer frame hanging over the bed.

"A sweet spot," said Cody, looking at the scene with his hands on his hips. "What are we looking for? It's not likely we'll find any poison here, if that's what killed him."

"Well, aside from that speech, which I think was mainly to enhance his credentials as a way to sell his editorial services, we know what he was doing. Barlow's services were touted in the brochure as the best route to New York publication. Let's start there." The publicity for the conference had also billed him as one of the less featured, but still key, speakers, without mentioning his intended subject. It highlighted instead his five-hour extra-cost workshop, following the main conference sessions, on writing "literary fiction." My eyebrows went up—what was this? From the paragraph following, I learned that it was a separate, higher art form than the more pedestrian genre fiction—like mysteries, science fiction, romance, or practically anything that regularly sold in large quantities in paperback, or at airport kiosks. From a private handout I'd seen at his speech, he was also offering to meet with potential or existing clients at times to be arranged, in order to "bring their work to a state of publication readiness without compromise."

So, as I interpreted it, he was offering to bring literary qualities to genre fiction, because this was a genre fiction conference. Did mystery writers harbor a secret lust to make real literature out of their low-rent product? Would Barlow make their mystery more publishable because it read like Hemingway or Grahame Greene? Clearly, much of this was beyond me.

From the little we had seen and heard I could believe that Barlow hadn't ever compromised, and had died in a state of literary grace. His soul would have gone directly to wherever the souls of writers and their teachers go, with no fuss or risky scene of judgment. Possibly his eternal destination would resemble a library of some kind. My guess was that, like the Zacher Agency, people in Barlow's position weren't paid to participate in the conference either. They may have had some help with lodging or travel expenses, but they were mainly in attendance to troll for business, or publicize their books if they were authors. Someone like the keynote speaker, Ruth Bendickson, would have been paid a fee and had her expenses covered as well. The improvised bookstore below ground outside the conference chambers prominently featured her books, as we saw when we walked down to the end of the hallway. It had no natural illumination. Writers of lesser reputation, the other presenters, and longtime supporters of the conference, were allowed to sell their books too, but from less well lit tables around the periphery. When I walked through, comparing the mass of covers with Maya's only book, many looked amateurish.

The arrangement of the bookstore conveyed a feeling of distinctly Orwellian hierarchies; places were provided for the more equal and the less equal. Each participant would have been clear on his or her degree of comparative equality based on proximity to the bright lighting. Electricity can be expensive here and you don't want to waste it.

Entering the Barlow speech, we'd been confronted at the door by a short, fussy woman showing too much cleavage for that time of morning. Her nametag identified her as Lola Barker, Staff. She had a round face and glasses pointed like wings at the outer corners in a way I hadn't seen for some time. Maybe that style was back again in the States. A cord at the ends of the bows kept them from fleeing. Her stated interest was in our credentials and in our legitimate (or not) reason for trying to attend Mr. Barlow's lecture on adverbs. I got the feeling she would have recognized and ruthlessly culled out any adverb herself, had she encountered one and recognized it. Her right hand was carried in an oddly rigid posture, as if it had been poised too long over the *delete* key on her computer, and frozen permanently in that pose. This may also have characterized her view of life, or maybe it was only her habit of pointing downward at everything. Looking at her, I felt I was getting ahead of myself, but I was also feeling a weird vibe from her. It was probably nothing, but the conference was clearly off to an awkward start. I tried to clear my mind of such speculations, because we were now looking for physical evidence.

Cody launched a search of Barlow's closet while I went for the desk and the nightstand. The latter contained only a Gideon Bible, in Spanish, and a blunt, well-used pencil with an eraser worn flat to its metal ring. Its yellow paint was slightly chewed. The desk, and the stack of papers on top of it, gave me three stained and dog-eared manuscripts, several New York newspapers, and a notebook with only a few blank pages remaining. I flipped through to find it had client records, including contact information, critical comments, and accumulating charges. This was the prize. In addition, I found a small sheaf of documents held together with a flaccid rubber band. They included the hotel check-in, air and shuttle reservations to LaGuardia, a single-sheet room service menu, and an estimate from a local dentist for a whopping 52,300 pesos. My eyebrows went up as I calculated this to be $4200 at current exchange rates. That was a lot of money in México, where my annual property taxes on Quebrada are the equivalent of $197. I held it up to Cody as he emerged from the closet. He studied it for a moment before his eyebrows went up at the total.

"Barlow must've had a lot of teeth. More than I do."

"Some of them were doomed, apparently, even aside from the two the lectern demolished. What did you get?"

"The man must also have had a seamstress in his neighborhood that he kept busy. I saw a lot of repairs to his clothes, and nothing that looked new. His alternate pair of shoes had been re-heeled in the same prosthetic way as the ones he was wearing."

"I've got three manuscripts and a fat notebook. I think that's where our case is."

"Do we even have a case?"

"The man was murdered, Cody, don't you think? We'll have a case once we get through all his stuff."

"We can't copy all of that."

"That's why we're taking it with it us."

"And Delgado would say?"

I could feel his resistance, but I wasn't going to help him amplify it.

"Nothing, because at this point, he doesn't know. If he doesn't know, he doesn't care. We can tell him more if he decides to investigate. If he doesn't think it's a crime, we can do what we want with this information. What the hell, we already gave him our list of front-row witnesses. We're upright citizens, serving the law enforcement community *pro bono*; do we have to draw him a picture?"

This last clause was something my dad used to say when no one understood him, which was not a rare event. There are times now when it still has the proper ring to it. If Delgado decided to proceed based on the lab tests from the autopsy, then we could reconvene and bring him up to date. Why apologize if he'd never been interested until that point? We'd always cooperated with him, and he'd be happy to look at our files. I still thought Barlow had been poisoned, and I didn't have to be able to prove it to ask why, or who might have done it. This was our tenth case, if it was a case at all, and at a certain point, I felt I could trust my instincts—that was my goal in any investigation, as it was in painting. I knew Cody had always trusted his, even though they seemed a little iffy here, and he was alive and prosperous as a result.

We finished with an examination of the tiny bathroom. The mirror over the sink was marked on the backside with dark, irregular mold-like blotches, as if a different world bloomed back there, one you would want to keep at arm's length. On the door hung a cotton hotel robe, and in front of it, a red silk robe. It was a luxury that gave me some insight into who Barlow thought he was when he was alone—or maybe it was for when he wasn't alone. The rest of his clothes were nondescript and well worn. In the wastebasket I saw two empty wine bottles from a Chilean vineyard. I recognized the label; they were inexpensive, but decent quality. They meant nothing special; in San Miguel good buys in Chilean wines abound. They might have been the same vineyard Barlow drank at home. Cody shuffled through his medications. Aside from the over-the-counter remedies, like aspirin and sinus tablets, he found a prescription bottle of Digoxin from a New York City pharmacy.

"This is for heart problems," he said. "I've seen it before. But again, the manner of his collapse didn't suggest a coronary, and I've seen more than a few of them." There was nothing more of interest in the bathroom that we could see without lab work.

We gathered up the evidence, such as it was, consisting only of Barlow's notebook, and put it into a tote bag Maya had bought when she signed us up for the conference. Walking away from this tawdry affair, emerging onto the bright, chaotic life of the Ancha de San Antonio, I wasn't ready to judge Barlow's life or death. On the surface it looked, for all his pretense at the conference, like he'd been the victim of no more than another routine crime, one that could not be inflated or justified by a "higher" view of literature or the arts. We'd had cases in the past where the crime had been committed for the highest of motives, but that didn't appear to be the case here, at least from what we had so far. My guess was that the solution, when it came, would probably be a gritty one.

I knew that Maya was still absorbed in the conference presentations, so Cody and I left for my house on Quebrada to spend some time with Justus Barlow's notebook. I was excited at the prospect—it had the well-used look of something he'd held to his heart every day and taken to bed with him at night.

The morning was still brilliant and promising, so we sat out on the *loggia*, behind a row of three arches of mellow buff-colored *cantera* limestone. The garden was looking more enthusiastic since the rains had appeared again, earlier than usual, if only briefly. I didn't have any on my property, but around us among the neighbors, the jacarandas had erupted in full bloom, seventy-five foot trees whose entire crown was covered with blue-violet flowers. Cody donned his reading glasses and scanned the notebook while I started a pot of coffee for us in the kitchen. I was back out in a minute and we examined it together.

Barlow's style of organization appeared to be rudimentary. Each time a new client came aboard he filled out an opening page with contact data and a few notes about what her goals were and the project she was working on. I say she, because in every case his clients were women. The book went back almost seven years and covered forty-nine clients.

"I wonder what else he did to live," said Cody. "Forty-nine clients over that period don't add up to a real income unless they were paying him more than $10,000 apiece. Is that likely?"

"I doubt it. How many clients have paid us that much? Only one."

"Good point."

Barlow was charging $85 an hour, keeping track in detail of all the meetings and phone conversations, besides reading the original manuscript and its revisions. Looking at his totals, he always rounded up to the nearest whole hour at the end of a session. Sixty-three minutes went down as two hours in his tally. But still, flipping through at random, I saw no billings that approached $10,000 in total. What was Barlow doing for lunch money? How was he paying his electric bill? And he lived in the Village, which I thought wasn't cheap. Apparently he wasn't fluent in computer skills—most people would've had this material on a laptop. The notebook, like all the notations on the manuscripts we'd left back in the room, was done with a blunt pencil, often faint and illegible. You'd think for that kind of hourly rate he'd furnish a printed copy.

Early on, from about six years back, we found an interesting entry; a new client named Ruth Bendickson. Barlow didn't note that she had a Ph.D. and preferred to be addressed with her title. Even more interesting was that her manuscript in progress was titled *These Things Are Mine.* Cody didn't see anything wrong with this, but I did.

"Maya told me the titles of Ruth Bendickson's books," I said. "They're called *Rachel's Folly*, *Rachel's Loves*, and *Rachel's Revenge*. It was a trilogy of mysteries, all connected in a personal way to Rachel's lifestyle and her love life. The concept was that disaster followed her, and she took it in stride and solved whatever came up. Part of the charm for the romance readers was that the crimes she investigated always intruded on her personal life, and she handled that too. I even glanced at the covers in the bookstore as we walked into the Barlow talk. There was nothing about *things*."

Cody shrugged reasonably. "So, the first one could have been retitled, or simply abandoned as a bad start. What does Barlow have for comments about her? Did he recognize the coming greatness?"

I scanned through Ruth Bendickson's opening pages. "Cut prologue entirely—go straight into the action. No explanations. Fuck the backstory, it doesn't matter. Who cares about little girls? Weak premise. Language is often stilted, too academic. Cut out the passive voice; it's for victims, not heroines. Sylvia needs to be more sensuous from page one. She touches things, smells things, hears things that others don't, and she even touches herself at inappropriate times. Make it SENSUAL! Make it a winner! Or just move on? This manuscript is worse than doubtful, but it could take up more sessions if she stays with it."

"OK. The guy wasn't shy about stating his opinions."

"We saw that before he died," I said. "Anyway, who is Sylvia?"

"She could have changed that name too. Was Ruth Bendickson already an academic when she signed up for this stream of abuse?"

I went back to her opening page. "Right, she was professor of creative writing at Bolton College, just as she is now."

"Wow. You'd think she'd have known most of this before she hooked up with Barlow. So what does she teach, if not the techniques of writing?"

"I don't know, writing theory? Doers do, but non-doers teach. I can tell you this: in painting, people who teach theory don't know how to paint. People who paint are often ignorant of theory because it's all in the eye and the hand, not the mind. They usually couldn't tell you verbally what they do. Maybe Dr. Ruth was nervous about making the transition from teacher to writer."

"I have a theory about the murder already, but it's preliminary."

"At this point, everything is preliminary."

Cody leaned back into his wicker chair and folded his arms while I poured the coffee. The chair creaked in mild protest at his weight and the shift in his center of gravity. I had seen this body language before when he was about to deliver a speculative analysis of the crime. It was never more than a preliminary guess at this point.

"This could be a simple revenge killing. Like a painter who's been harshly critiqued, Ruth Bendickson is a writer who's ego-involved with her work. She put it out to Barlow for help and, to her great surprise, she got slammed. Because she teaches it, and has some status in the field, she's even more vulnerable when she gets negative comments, even though she's not used to actually writing herself. I would think a book doctor has some of the same behavioral guidelines as a medical doctor, or should have. Do no harm, that's part of the Hippocratic oath, right?

As a professor of the skill Ruth is also now trying to practice, she has more to lose than Barlow's other clients. His comments could damage her reputation if they were made public. When she came in looking for help from him, even some confirmation of how good she was, she needed to know at a minimum how much better she was than her students. She was expecting a few tweaks here and there to perfect her book, perhaps, because he's got to give her something for her money. Instead, Barlow smacked her hard. He probably told her to forget it, if he followed his comments in the notebook."

"But then why would she wait almost six years to kill him? You'd think her anger would've cooled by now, particularly after three bestsellers. She could forgive a lot at that point. You're describing a crime of passion, specifically outrage. If anything, Ruth went on to prove him wrong, so she won the debate hands down. What better vindication could she have than that? Where's the anger now, when it turned out that Barlow was just a vindictive schmuck? And years ago at that, when it doesn't really matter anymore in terms of what happened later?"

"I see your point, but maybe running into him here got her going again."

"I don't know," I said, "it feels thin to me.

What if he was right about her work, as it was at that time with *These Things Are Mine*? And why didn't she collect this notebook, if she killed him?"

"Simple," he said. "Because we got to it before she did. We're the pros here, we know what to do. If this is her first murder, there's some improvisation involved. You know how it often goes. With the first one, you don't see it coming, but you feel threatened so you have to do it. Then some small detail pops up that you overlooked. If what you missed comes up later it could point a finger at you, so the second murder happens mainly to cover-up the loose ends from the first. And so on. A lot of it is about planning, or the lack of it. Spontaneity is dangerous in a murder."

"Since we're now scanning that lost detail, I feel like we have targets on our chests."

"As always, but more likely on our backs. So what?" He shrugged. I didn't ever remind him that he'd been shot in the leg on our first case.

I skipped ahead to the last three clients. I had memorized their names; they were the ones whose manuscripts we'd left behind on the desk in Barlow's room. For him to have brought them along, these three clients were probably in attendance. I suddenly recalled the smudged, pencil-written notes on all of them. Certainly the $85 an hour those women paid him was not buying much clarity. I'd estimated when I had glanced through those manuscripts that fully a third of the notations were indecipherable. Was no one complaining? Was no one feeling taken advantage of? Maybe they were, but Barlow didn't take note of it.

"Taking these three manuscript people from the oldest in terms of when they started with Barlow," I said, "we have Denny Frost up first, divorced and still single, from Athens, Georgia. The word *divorced* is underlined in the second line. A note in the margin adds, *attending conf. Set up meeting. Several?*

"Her name would be Denise, do you think?"

"Probably." I went on to summarize from Barlow's notes. "From her own statement, Denny Frost's project is a literary memoir, fictionalized as needed. She sees herself as deeply embedded in the mainstream of the Georgia, Alabama, and Mississippi writing heritage; sensitive people—often women—who have taken up the Southern tradition of story-telling, and refined it into a vehicle that lends meaning and clarity to their lives. As an extremely feminine person, she loves having a masculine name. It plays against type, one of the writing devices she favors most. She prefers to be addressed as 'Miss

Denny.' It doesn't sound like a mystery to me. Maybe her life is mysterious to her."

"Wow. I think I'd like to read that."

"Barlow couldn't agree less. Let me quote: 'Yet, in spite of these lofty ambitions, she furnishes another sloppy venture into an emotional quicksand of no return, indistinguishable from its mewing litter-mates in an overpopulated genre. It brings new levels of nuance to self-indulgence, but never to style or relevance. While Miss Denny's language can at times be fine—possibly when she's been hitting the Southern Comfort—it is often wasted in the service of a shallow, self-indulgent mind clinging to illusions about the past that others of greater skill would long ago have abandoned. This is ineptitude cloaked in gentility. In Frost's work, Scarlett O'Hara meets *Peyton Place*. Rather than driving Miss Denny, in this circuit of the track, we are more likely to be her first pit stop."

"Wow! Still, I do enjoy women like that," said Cody. "They fill an emotional void for me where only shell casings and microscope slides have been rattling around in a space much too large and for far too long. I think we should talk to her." I couldn't bring myself to remind him of his current connection with Sheila Roper, the psychic, since whenever I got launched in speculating about some interesting woman, he never brought up Maya's name.

"And we will certainly talk to Denny Frost. I wonder now about the underlining here of the word *divorced*, and then there's a final note, somewhat removed, almost a footnote, as if Barlow had discovered this later, but still on the first page of comments. He adds, '*Comes from money*.'"

"Then we should look up Frost. For starters, had Miss Denny taken back her family name, or did she do well from divorcing her Frost husband? In other words, where did the money come from?"

"No suggestion of the answer to that in the notebook," I said. "Barlow may not have cared. Money is money, and I'm starting to think he had developed a nose for it. But I'm also getting something else here. Barlow was a *predator*. Why is it only women writers who are in need of saving? Maybe at five-foot-seven, he didn't easily dominate men, and he turned them away as clients, even though he could've used their business. You saw him at the end. What woman would want him?"

"I'm no writer, OK? But I can imagine it's often connected to ego. You're putting your innermost thoughts out there for anyone to read, right? You're saying things you'd never say in conversation. You wouldn't tell them to your parents. So what happens if you get pounded, laughed at, even ridiculed, when you show them to Barlow in a manuscript?"

"That response, of preying on your hesitation," I said, "must have been his stock in trade. That's how he made his money. Say you're a woman writer who comes in—he humiliates you, puts you in a hole, and leads you on at the same time. Then he offers you the cure, the road out of the misery he'd amplified, or even planted in some cases. By that time, he already knows your dream in detail. You gave it to him in trust. In return, he gave you success by the hour at his standard rate, as the process went on, and the number of hours would constantly need to be increased. It was determined by how long you could be made to suffer and pay. Your redemption was always just a step or two ahead, yet oddly out of reach."

"That sounds like it's structured the same as a church. So, did he do that to Ruth Bendickson too? She had the nerve to move way past him if he did. Did she just shake him off?"

"I'm speculating that he must've done it to all of his clients. That was his process, his machine. It chewed everyone up. Remember, they came in questioning what they had to offer. They began by exhibiting their weakness to him. They tell him, 'Here's my problem, doctor. I don't know how to get past it.'"

I flipped back toward the first section of the notebook, through pages of demeaning comments, looking for Dr. Ruth, and landed somewhat earlier than her arrival, at the final page of a woman named Amy Wendt, from Bethpage, Long Island. She was an instructor in freshman English at Briarcliffe College, not a rank with any prestige, nor a job with much satisfaction. What caught my eye farther down the page was an oversize exclamation point following the phrase beginning in block capitals, "DEAD! Who the bloody hell is going to pay me?" This was the final entry on Amy Wendt's time tally page.

"His client is dead, and that's his first thought?" said Cody in an ashen tone.

This needed no response, and I turned back to Amy Wendt's critique file. At twenty-six years old, she was already a writer who'd produced two novels. Barlow had looked at both and characterized them as better than most. "Listen to this: 'A solid narrative line. Moves out of the opening paragraph like a sprinter in heat. Lead characters are formidable, but the secondary group could use some work, maybe a lot. Has she made them too weak, thinking to give greater support to the main ones? If so, it's over-done. Focus on this aspect. She needs help. Punish her a bit—she can take it. It's close to being ready to publish, but the closer it is, the more time and work it needs, not less. That's the paradox of near victory. Hammer this home."

Several more pages followed in the same style. Cody looked at me like I'd lost a few IQ points while I read the first part. "Barlow really says that? The closer it is to being ready, the more time and work it needs?"

"Yes, exactly that."

"So if I bring in a very rough piece that's a long way from being publishable, then it's not going to need much work? That guy must have been *loco*. Did he think his clients would really buy that?"

"Apparently," I said. "But, don't forget, we haven't seen these manuscripts."

"Then I wonder what killed Amy Wendt? He's got her contact info on the first of her pages, right? We can figure it out later. It's more than five years ago now, so other than underlining the preda-tor aspect of Barlow's personality, I doubt it has any-thing to do with this case. Who's the next of our three suspects?"

I went on to the second of Barlow's clients,

a woman named Dina Bauer. She was working on a book titled *Less Than Zero*. I knew that title had already been used, but you can't copyright a title, according to Maya.

"The victim is frozen to death?" suggested Cody.

CHAPTER FOUR

As we started probing Dina Bauer's records, I had the usual mixed feelings about information that pointed us in a variety of directions. Almost every new case started like that. My cell phone went off as we sat there. It was Chad Metcalf on the other end. I had the sense that things were heating up at the conference management office. Did he suspect we were already on the case?

"Zacher, we have to talk."

I found his abruptness a little startling, but he didn't live here and had never had a chance to absorb the Méxican style of good manners. Possibly he hadn't noticed it.

"We can talk. When and where are you thinking?"

"I have an office at the Rosewood. It's on the first floor behind the lobby on the left. You can ask at the desk; they all know me. Shall we say in the next half hour? Sooner, if you can. This is important."

So Metcalf was in a rush, and I couldn't blame him. The conference was only a week in length, plus the extra premium sessions, and it had gotten off to a bad start on the first day.

"Do you know anything more?" I asked.

"No. That's why I want to talk to you people. I'm thinking we have to get a grip on this before it goes too far. Even if the facts aren't known yet, there's always the rumor mill to combat. I'll start my own if I have to; don't ever sell me short. I'm prepared to go the whole nine yards."

"We're at my house on Quebrada," I said. "It's only seven or eight blocks away. We'll be there in fifteen minutes."

"That was Metcalf, and he's worried," I told Cody after I hung up. "He's terrified of the publicity that might come from Barlow's death. You know what he's going to want."

"Sure. He'll want us to put a lid on it."

"He's going to ask us to be his personal Warren Commission. He'll tell us in advance what the outcome of our investigation will be. We'll need to say that Barlow died of natural causes. No one else was involved, and no crime was committed. We'll have a moment of silence while we all close ranks to mourn the passing of a dear friend, an irreplaceable asset to the literary community. Then we'll get back to work."

"Of course," he said. "This will be like when Jack Elgin hired us to prove he didn't kill his wife in the Jack and Jill case."

"Exactly, it all depends on the scope of our assignment. Let's get him to spell out what he wants in great detail."

"But we still do what we have to do. Metcalf's instructions will only frame our report."

Twenty minutes later, a bellhop led us from the bright lobby of the Rosewood to a corridor off the back wall, where a series of five business offices supported temporary activities that were not announced on the doors. Chad Metcalf met us at the entrance to the third one.

"Come on in," he said, in a confidential tone, and closed the door behind us.

I introduced Cody, whom Metcalf hadn't met except anonymously at Barlow's collapse. Maya and I had both talked to him on the phone earlier, but never in person. The room was windowless and tight, with two armless chairs facing his desk, and a loveseat against one wall fronted by a coffee table. Opposite, a small bar offered a coffee maker next to a miniscule square sink, and a liquor cabinet with a half-size refrigerator below. I was surprised to find him housed in this modest fashion, but it may have been his way of being less accessible to the crowd downstairs.

His maroon sport coat, worthy of a football or golf broadcaster, hung on the back of his desk chair, and his shirtsleeves were rolled up.

"Thanks for coming in. Did anyone see you?"

"The bellhop," said Cody. We'd agreed on the way over that we'd say nothing about our visit to Barlow's room.

Metcalf shrugged. "You can see the problem I've got now. We work hard at having a polished, upscale image, which is what good mystery writing is all about, of course, and now this. I've got to put a lid on it before it hits the news media with some splashy headline, particularly the American press. They'll drag me through the mud for scheduling the conference in México, saying how I invited this by disregarding the risk. They're such whores now it makes me sick. They'll say anything that'll sell a paper."

"What's the remedy?" asked Cody. When he wanted, he could bring a neutral tone into his voice that contained absolutely no content for anyone to read. This was one of those moments.

I observed the cleft in Metcalf's chin flatten slightly, exposing a less tanned area within as his cheeks pulled upward and tightened in a tense grin. His eyes grew smaller as he shook his head, yet not a hair on his head moved. "Damage control." He spit it out.

"We're not publicists," Cody responded, "in fact, we always avoid publicity."

"Of course you're not. And we do have a publicist in New York that I've already talked to. Naturally, he's the very first one I called when Justus fell over backwards this morning—after the ambulance, of course. He's already framing an assortment of responses to this, depending on what you can find out. I mean, the man's body wasn't even cold when I got him started on it. Sally Field uses our New York guy too, by the way, so you know he's *that* good." Metcalf's thumb and middle finger rose in contact with each other as if ready to snap, but they didn't. "Don't worry; we are so ready to spin this our own way. We've absolutely got to find out what happened so we can see whether the facts have any bearing on our position. I would've launched our response already, but I don't want to get blindsided on this. My first choice would be that we spin it that Barlow was so excited to see the overflow crowd that he had a heart attack. Do you think we could get some local doc to put out a statement to that effect, even if it cost a few pesos? What do you call it here, *dinero*?" He rubbed the index finger and thumb of his right hand together.

"He gave his life for his art," suggested Cody, nodding, instead of answering Metcalf's question.

"You're really all over this," I said. The amazement in my voice was genuine as I tried hard to imagine Barlow dying from joy.

"That's my job, Paul, and I take it very seriously."

"Then what we need to have at the outset," I said, "is a clear set of instructions, a task list, if you will, that defines point for point what you would like the Zacher Agency to do. It's what you're going to pay for." That last sentence was what Maya would've wanted me to say.

"Of course." Metcalf pressed his palms together and brought their edges up to his pursed lips. He leaned back in his black leather chair. He opened his mouth to speak and then stopped. Had the office been larger, he would have had room to put his feet up on the desk, crossed ankle over ankle. Briefly, he looked at the ceiling as if composing his thoughts. "I would ask the Zacher Agency to prove that my poor friend Justus Barlow died of quite natural causes." He surveyed our reaction. "I'm serious. He was younger than I am by a few months. Don't you find that alarming?" He looked mainly at Cody, who had just turned sixty, as he said this. I hadn't reached forty yet, although I could see it looming in the shadows down the road.

Cody regarded Chad Metcalf with what I describe as his 'dead fish' look. It was like that of a carp washed up on a riverbank, and it was one of his most effective interrogation devices. His eyes didn't move; they only waited in blank anticipation.

"And do you think death by natural causes was the case here?" he said. "Because we were present when it happened. It appeared somewhat different to me."

Metcalf looked back at him for a moment, but no one I've encountered so far in this shifty business has been able to stare Cody down, and the conference director's eyes wavered before moving on to objects less formidable. Yet he continued in the same vein.

"But you were not sitting in the front row, as I'm told. In fact, you were somewhat back in the crowd, and along the edge, where your view of the platform would've been partially obscured. At the same time, I think that might provide you with an opportunity for better objectivity, if you know what I mean. Eyewitnesses are notoriously unreliable, not that you people were in this instance. Isn't that true, in your experience, Cody? I'm sure you organized many lineups in your time." As if that time was long past, perhaps when J. Edgar Hoover was still with the FBI, just at the outer limits of recollection. This was not an argument designed to win Cody over, however.

Cody Williams was less vulnerable to being patronized than practically any man I've ever known, except by Maya, whose flirting could raise an active pulse in the dead. Cody had always had a special weakness for her. I understood this well because I shared it, so I didn't object. Besides, she eagerly encouraged him. For her, conversation was a contact sport, at least with men she thought attractive.

"And if it turns out that Justus Barlow was murdered?" I asked. "What instructions would you have for the Zacher Agency in that case?"

Metcalf pondered this for a moment. "My first instinct is to say I don't want to hear about it, but that hardly serves the interest of the conference, does it? I think I would have to know, *very* privately. Then, depending on who did it, we could figure out how to position it."

I glanced at Cody, but he didn't need my cue to remain silent about what else we'd do if it did turn out to be murder. Clearly, we'd also tell Diego Delgado *very* privately. We had helped Delgado and his judicial police as often as he'd helped us. We would never sacrifice that link for Chad Metcalf, who, like the local circuses that came though San Miguel from time to time, would soon be moving on, leaving a busy cleanup crew in his wake. I couldn't picture the Paul Zacher Agency behind one of those brooms.

"Did Barlow have any immediate family?" Cody asked.

"No, and he often lamented that fact. He once asked me, 'Who's going to bury me, Chad, when the time comes?' I told him I would."

"Once the body is released by the coroner in Guanajuato," I said, "you'll have twenty-four hours to bury him, cremate him, or get his remains out of México. That's the law." Hearing myself say this, I thought it sounded insensitive, but Metcalf didn't react to it. Maybe insensitivity was one of those things that didn't cause a blip on his radar.

"Did he have any enemies that you knew of?" asked Cody.

"Justus? Oh, I suppose some people must

have envied him and wanted to take his place. Who wouldn't? There was no one like him in this business. He had the knack like few others ever would."

I nodded solemnly.

"One more thing then," said Cody, giving nothing away. "While I recognize that your interest is best served if Barlow died from natural causes, at the same time, do you have any information that might suggest otherwise? It could save us some time, and we're paid by the hour."

"None at all. And that reminds me—here's your retainer. I think you said $500?"

He slid a check across the desk to me. His business card was clipped to it. I was surprised that he hadn't put it in an envelope the way most clients did. Showing us out, he said, "I'll call the conference registration people downstairs and tell them to give you whatever help you need. And by the way, good luck tomorrow morning. I know you'll have a lively reception for your session. I'll be there to introduce you promptly at ten o'clock."

"Might as well get started," Cody said as we walked back out through the lobby. We went downstairs to the registration desk and got the contact information for all three of Barlow's manuscript clients. Cody phoned Miss Denny Frost on the way back up through the amphitheater outside. We were lucky, since not every U.S. cell phone worked in San Miguel. Hers did.

Two hours later we met Denny Frost at the edge of the main level courtyard of the Rosewood, where a dozen tables were distributed in strings of three in the shade of the long *loggias*. White stone trim edged the crimson walls at the doors and windows, and the walkways divided the courtyard into four wedges with a tiled fountain in the center. Only two other tables were occupied, both beyond easy earshot. She was staring off into the manicured spaces with a cup of tea at her left hand. An orange and white cloth covered the wrought iron table. The time was just after three in the afternoon, during a break from the rigorous sessions inside. Our first suspect was not wearing a hoopskirt with a square neckline and enticing cleavage, but nonetheless, she projected a charmingly feminine antebellum persona. Her wavy hair was deep auburn, pulled back from her delicate features, and her pale skin was lightly freckled. She looked happy to be sitting in the shade.

Miss Denny wore a jade and gold bracelet with a belted sheath dress that came to the top of her knees as she rose from the table to greet us. From the slight crinkle at the corners of her green eyes I placed her age at early to mid thirties. On her left hand flashed a solitaire cut diamond that looked to be at least one and a half carats. Her nails were elaborately done, with an almost art deco graphic repeated on each one, and they looked too long to type with. Even so, we knew she had to be a writer.

"I'm Denny Frost," she said. "Which one of you is Cody? I believe it must be *you*." Her expression and tone both suggested this was the best surprise of her day so far, and not likely to be topped by any other. Her lips seemed caught in a kiss. Cody flushed to the roots of his sandy hair when she said his name. She thrust out her hand, palm-downward, as if expecting him to press it to his mouth. When he took it in his own, he looked unsure what else he ought to be doing with it.

"Paul Zacher," I said. Miss Denny was still holding onto Cody's hairy paw as she turned to look at me as I continued. "I'm sorry about Justus Barlow. I know you were working with him on a memoir project, and I appreciate your taking the time to talk with us." Establish a base line of sympathy straight out, I was thinking. She looked like a woman for whom relationships were usually personal, and often close.

"I don't mind—I don't care much about missing the next session, since it's about self-publishing. Fortunately, that's not a direction that *I* would ever have to take."

"Of course not," said Cody, as if he knew this for a certainty.

I noticed that she didn't respond to my sympathy.

"Anyway, I suspect somebody murdered that pore old boy," she said sweetly, with a smile that invited us to share her ironic sense of justice, even when it was irregular in its methods. "I'd say he damn well had it coming. Please have a seat." Cody and I sat down after she did, and we waited for her to go on. "You probably think I did it: certainly I had at least as much motive as anyone." If justice hadn't already been blind, her blazing smile might have brought that condition about.

"Never in a lifetime would we think that, and we don't even know yet that it was a murder," said Cody, gently batting her suggestion aside. His meaty hand displayed the subtlety of a butterfly wing. He was bidding up the game with a kind of pussycat look I'd never noticed on his broad face before. Maybe it was one he used with Maya when I wasn't around. I took the cue and kept silent. "In fact, I'm hoping it wasn't murder," he went on. "Anyway, we were able to have a look at your manuscript, and the level of sensitivity it displayed was not what you'd ever expect from the devious mind of a killer." Cody hadn't read even two sentences of it in Barlow's room, where we'd left it behind with the others. "For me, there was *way* too much finesse in the writing. Murder, something I've been around for a number of years—I won't even suggest how many—is a much cruder sport. I could show you my own bullet holes."

This was a bit too cozy for my taste, and much farther than our normal investigative techniques went in trying to win the confidence of a suspect. I felt like reminding him that she was half his age and a possible killer. Furthermore, I wasn't sure he ought to be letting on how much he was already on her side. Even Denny Frost herself was giving him a skeptical look.

"Do you have a specific reason for thinking Barlow might have been murdered?" I intervened, reluctant to go off the rails entirely. "Other than that he deserved it? That could apply to a number of people."

She looked at me coolly, folding her arms as

an ironic smile curled her lips. "Only that I've had my fill of men, if you catch my meaning, and Justus Barlow fancied himself—hard to imagine!—as next in line to go to bed with me." Both her palms went up as if to fend off his memory. "He apparently thought I was far more experienced than I really am. He brought up the subject of my divorce so many times I wished I'd never mentioned it—it was only background information that he'd requested at the beginning. As subtle as he thought himself, he completely missed the fact that I'd already gone over to the other team. I mean; he'd read the manuscript, hadn't he?"

"Team?" said Cody, perking up. Although he was six-foot-three, her statement had sailed over his head. Was he thinking of Green Bay or Oakland? I thought I knew what Denny Frost meant, and even as attractive as she was, I couldn't see her as a football cheerleader.

"Did Barlow come on to you directly?" I asked.

"So much so that I couldn't help but question how valuable his comments on my manuscript really were. For example, had the favorable ones, which were rare enough, only been prompted by his interest in sleeping with me? Of course, he was repulsive as a man, even more as a human being. I suppose some women might like that, but I don't. I don't care to be roughly handled. My private name for him was Gimpy, and I couldn't bear those big shoulder pads. I imagined them sewed not into his jackets, but into his tee shirts, so he must have had at least two sets. One he kept for Sunday." Cody gave her a sharp look that she didn't notice because she was trying not to laugh at her own image of Barlow. I thought she had nailed him.

Suddenly I had the recollection of myself straddling his hips that morning about to start CPR on him. I hadn't been eager to do the rescue breathing part, and I identified with her in that respect. I'd thought several times how lucky I'd been to have the young doctor rescue me at the right moment.

"So," I said, recalling Barlow's description of her work as an emotional quicksand, "did he like your manuscript?" At this point, I was wondering whether a better description for her terrain might be *briar patch*.

"To a point," she said, leaning toward me with one hand over the other, "although I'm not sure he understood it. He thought I should've included more detail about the circumstances of my divorce. Had I been, for example, unfaithful? Even with a series of different men? Most particularly, had I been caught in the act? He said that seeing the climactic breakdown that led up to it would've given it more dramatic tension. He was looking for some big sex scenes." Her index finger slowly traced the rim of her cup. "I hate scenes of any kind."

"And you had glossed over the divorce in your story?"

She nodded slowly. "You might say that. I omitted it outright. My book isn't about dramatic tension, it's about growth. The main tension is with the person I had pretended to be when I was married, and before. It begins with me walking out of the courthouse after signing the divorce decree, which is to say that it begins with me finally starting a new life on my own terms."

A glance at Cody told me he was starting to get what she meant.

"Are you thinking of doing a mystery when your memoir is finished? Is that why you came?" Cody asked.

"I don't know. Writing skills are universal. Whatever I can pick up here will apply as well to any books I do in the future. Good books are all about character and pace, suspense and surprise. That doesn't change much, unless you're doing cookbooks,

I suppose, or dictionaries."

"Did you feel you got your money's worth from Barlow's critiques?" I asked. Her comments had a familiar sound so far, based on Barlow's notebook.

"I had only paid him a $1000 retainer when I came on, and I guess that was about how much value I got. Not everything he said was useful. In fact, most of it wasn't."

Cody and I had seen this payment in the notebook, but subsequent time entries suggested she had run up a tab he was planning to bill at about $3100 more.

"What were your meetings like?"

"Well, until the conference, I had only spoken with him by phone on six or seven occasions for about an hour each time. We met three times down here. Once we had met face-to-face the first time, he began to insert a few upbeat comments, like how it was good that I wasn't using adverbs all the time. Then he'd say how attractive I was. He never did that on the phone."

"Did he ever try to touch you?" asked Cody.

Denny nodded slowly. "When he did, I'd pull back. Then he'd get nasty and stop looking me in the eye. Then he'd start saying the manuscript was emotionally self-indulgent." She picked up her spoon and stirred the tea for a moment, but didn't drink any more of it. "I thought of it as frank. Women do have emotional lives, I would say to him. They ought to be a valid subject. He mostly shrugged at that thought."

"Did you think that if you'd allowed him to get closer to you he would've thought more of the book?"

"That's how it felt, but I didn't care to test it. I only wanted to find a publisher. He said he could do that, once it was 'right'."

"So why did you put up with him at all?" said Cody. "He sounds like a buffoon."

Miss Denny shrugged and leaned back in her chair. "Two reasons. First, he'd been highly recommended to me by Chad Metcalf, who's kind of a legend in this business. He and Chad were old friends from Greenwich Village. They'd both been community organizers during Bill Clinton's first campaign. I thought if Chad was behind Barlow, he must have something more to offer, beyond what I was seeing at first. Maybe it would gradually emerge. You see, this isn't my first time at this conference. Last year, Chad urged me to get help from Barlow. I didn't do it immediately, but I thought about it for seven or eight months, and then I finally contacted him.

"The other reason was that a fair number of the comments Barlow made really did make sense to me, even though a lot of them didn't. I've been in several writers' work groups, and I've discovered that when you put your work out for criticism, you always have to pick through what people are saying about it because their motives and their level of sophistication differs. Now and then, when someone tells me an unpleasant truth, I get the feeling that I may have already known it at some level—but it's only when I hear it from someone else that I'm forced to come to terms with it. I can't dodge it anymore. I already knew that I have a tendency to ignore insights about myself that I don't want to deal with."

"Did you want to kill him?" said Cody, in the same tone as if asking whether she wanted to have lunch tomorrow.

Miss Denny nodded solemnly. "There were times when I absolutely did. He would greet me as 'Miss Denny Belle,' in this phony Rhett Butler accent. It was his way of mocking me, and I knew it. New Yorkers can be *very* superior, especially, I think, toward women from the South. At other times he had a foul nastiness of tone in his delivery that made me think he was scoring points on me in some way. Barlow was a crude man, and he loved to sneer.

His lip had a natural curl. I thought I'd heard it on the phone, and when I saw it in person I wasn't surprised. Maybe that was only for me, because I didn't want him to touch me, but that's why I said to you right away that someone had probably killed him. I may not look like it, but I have a thick skin. I'm not sure that was true of all his clients." She ended this with a broad smile, as if to dilute the effect of it. Her teeth were awfully white, maybe too white. I don't mind white teeth, but I don't care for glare when I look at someone's face.

"Did he ever let you look at the copy of your manuscript that he was using to write his comments on?" Cody asked.

"No. I haven't seen it. It was never in view in his hotel room when we got together, and he always spoke about it from memory."

"Weren't you nearly finished with your sessions by this time?" I asked. I had flipped through her manuscript to the end, and Barlow had marked almost all the pages.

"I thought so, but when I arrived here, he said we'd need to fit some more meetings in toward the end or even after the conference. He didn't care if that meant I'd have to stay on for a few more days, since he felt it was absolutely critical to the success of the book, and we were almost there."

"And you said?"

"Well, by that time I knew I was finished, even if he didn't. I'm not stupid, and I dislike repetition. We were going over the same issues again and again." Her face took on a fiery look as if reliving that moment. "I said flat-out that I would see the Yankees burning Atlanta again before I would do that. I told Barlow to wrap it up and give me the bill. He said he'd have to sit down and total up the hours from the beginning. Until he could do that, he couldn't even estimate how much it was."

Cody and I exchanged glances. In the notebook, Barlow had recalculated the total after every session. "Then he asked me if I didn't want the four free hours I was entitled to."

"Four free hours?" This took Cody by surprise and he frowned in disbelief. "That sounds a lot more like a lawn service promotion than professional manuscript editing."

"That was my reaction, too." She placed her hand delicately over his for a second. "He had never mentioned that before, and I saw it as a way of getting me to stay around so he could make another move on me. I can still see his pale, clammy hands, with those little clumps of dark hair between each knuckle. He chewed his fingernails too, by the way." Her lips tightened into a line.

"Sounds like your experience might find a place in another memoir. Did Barlow ever tell you what books he'd had a role in reshaping into best sellers?" I asked.

"Not specifically. First he said he never discussed his clients with each other, and later, when I brought it up again, he said that the list was too long to recite, and he didn't want me to have to pay him for more time."

"Didn't this set off alarms in your head?"

"Yes, but Chad Metcalf had told me that Barlow was hugely successful in getting books ready to be sold to New York publishers. That was all that mattered to me. Do you think he took advantage of me?"

"At this point," Cody said, "you're only out your time, if you think you got your money's worth from the deposit."

"When did you see him last?" I asked.

"Last night at eight o'clock as I walked out of his hotel room."

We left Miss Denny seated at the table with her chin resting on the back of one hand as she pensively stirred her cold cup of tea. A waiter hovered unnoticed near her back. I could see that we must have stimulated a stream of recollections of her time inside the labyrinthine corridors of the Justus Barlow experience.

I was starting to sense an incestuous interconnection threading its way through the conference. The same names kept coming up: Bendickson with Barlow years ago, Chad and Barlow with the Clinton campaign, Chad in charge of everything, Bendickson the keynote speaker. Was there yet another link between Chad and Ruth Bendickson we hadn't yet discovered? I wouldn't have been at all surprised if one turned up. I suddenly wondered whether Barlow was in attendance at every conference, and I made a note to retrieve the list of their previous featured speakers if it was still available online.

"I think we should cross Denny Frost off the list," said Cody. He almost sounded relieved as we emerged under the carport at the Rosewood entry.

"But can we do that so quickly? We haven't talked to anyone else yet."

"You don't think we can? Did you see her as a steel magnolia, with claws under the delicate petals?"

"Not that, exactly, but thorns, maybe. You can't blame her. A lot of delicate flowering plants have thorns. It's not only roses, think of the bougainvillea here."

We walked down the driveway to the edge of Calle Nemesio Diez and paused at the edge of the cobblestones. I tried to phrase what I was about to say in a way that wouldn't sound hostile toward Denny Frost, because I didn't feel that way toward her.

"I both saw and heard what she wanted me to think about her, Cody. I didn't dislike her, but I did get her message, and it made me wonder what was behind it. She's not a woman that people would want to keep their distance from; on the contrary, most people she meets would probably take a liking to her right away. That includes me. But when someone confesses in practically her first sentence that she'd thought about murdering a person who was just murdered, for me that's way too easy. It's a smokescreen in itself—the opposite of a confession. We're meant to think that no guilty person would ever volunteer those evil thoughts."

Cody looked uneasily down the street. We stepped aside as a shuttle van with tourist plates pulled into the Rosewood drive. I understood him well enough to know he was questioning his own objectivity, which he could readily do with no protest. "I can understand that argument, and I see why you'd say that, but I bought it all the same."

"You wanted to buy it, once you'd met her. Denny's a charmer. You're from Illinois. Maybe women of the Old South instinctively have your number. I can see it myself. She'll look you in the eye and put her hand on your cheek as she talks to you. Maybe not literally, but that's how it feels. Or she might sometimes really do that. When she's listening to you, she's close enough to be a little more in your personal space than if she was from New Hampshire or Toronto. But a little bit more into your personal space is where you'd want her. There's more connect-edness in a conversation with Miss Denny."

Cody shrugged and shook his head with a sigh. "I guess there was an element of that, but I've seen a lot of criminal types, Paul, and they rarely look or act like Denny Frost. At the same time I real-ize that's not enough to go on."

"But think about the world of writers, the world we're thrust into here. It's foreign terrain to both of us. These people are all storytellers. In any court, you'd fight to keep them off the witness stand. I suspect they can tell you a story about themselves as quickly as about any other character that comes to mind. Inventing things is their stock-in-trade, and it all has to be credible enough that they can stand up on the page. Yet, every single one of their characters comes out of their own head. They themselves are all of the people they write about, even when those fictional people are also based on someone real."

He thought about this for a moment. "But Denny Frost is working on a memoir. Isn't that non-fiction?"

"From what I've been hearing and seeing at this conference and in Barlow's notes, I wonder if nonfiction really exists? I'm reminded of the way I process the reality I see in front of me into paint on the canvas. What I do isn't 'true' in any objective sense, and although the viewer easily connects with it because he recognizes it as familiar, I still always make it impossible for him to forget that it's really no more than oil paint on canvas. That's why I prefer a crude weave to paint on—the fabric is always undeniable through the image."

"You're saying that what she's doing, what they're all doing here, is fiction, even though it looks like nonfiction. Even when it's labeled *nonfiction*."

"I guess I am, and it doesn't make our job any easier."

CHAPTER FIVE

The International Mystery Writers' Conference had scheduled a cocktail party that evening to introduce Dr. Ruth Bendickson to the participants. I'd seen no information posted at the Rosewood conference desk before we left suggesting that Justus Barlow's death was going to cancel it or cause it to be rescheduled. Knowing Chad Metcalf's need for damage control, I suspected there was no way he'd ever change it—the show had to go on. Carrying on in the face of adversity would be his new mantra, no matter what it cost him personally. Maya was stewing over her wardrobe when I got home after our meeting with Miss Denny. I hadn't seen her since we parted in the lobby of the Rosewood that morning.

"Today was almost worthless. No one could talk about anything except *The Death of the Adverb Killer* speech, as they're calling it now. The presenters were tearing their hair out."

"Well, we're hired."

"I expected that. We need a case anyway, not that this is the way to get one. What's your take on it? I know you've got one."

"I'd say murder by poison." I filled her in on everything we'd done so far. She'd already heard everything she ever wanted to know about Barlow's death on the podium.

"You're in motion. Now I feel like the murderer is someone I was sitting next to today."

"Probably. If it is a participant, she'd want to blend right back into the crowd."

"She? Is there something you didn't tell me?"

"All of Barlow's clients were women. I did forget to tell you that part."

"That would fit with poison. I'm going to need some new outfits if we're going to be getting into high society like this affair tonight."

"Now we're detectives to the stars? You still look pretty good." She gave me a withering look. Maybe there was a conference session on adjective enhancement in personal relationships I could attend.

"That's what I mean. Pretty good isn't going to cut it tonight. I need to be stunning."

"Too late to shop now. Let's go to the Tuesday Market next week. We'll get you a pair of new jeans with those sparkly sequin shields on the butt."

"How was Denny Frost?" she asked, staring into the sparsely populated interior of her armoire. This house is too old to have closets. They would've been high tech, cutting edge, when it was built.

"In a word, fetching. Cody was impressed by her."

"Was she fetching to you?"

"Not as much, but I did like her."

"But Cody's got Sheila now."

"I know. Denny Frost isn't going to give him any encouragement, or me either, for that matter."

"Isn't he a little old for her? Most of the people at the conference are younger."

"Yes, but that's not the problem. Denny works for the other side."

"She's a spy?" Maya's eyebrows went up, reaching for her hairline, and she looked directly at me for the first time.

"No, she's a loyal, Southern woman of the most sophisticated bearing. She just doesn't like men in that way, anymore. She must have once, because she was married for a time, but she's clear that things have changed. I think her memoir is about reinventing herself."

"Oh, OK. Maybe she never liked men. Some women work hard at doing what's expected of them. More than most men do, I think."

I saw something in this that I didn't want to confront at that moment. "She'd probably like you, especially like that." Maya was pulling off her black linen slacks. Nothing sparkled on their back pockets.

"I'm going for serious casual tonight."

"What's that?"

"An emerald silk top and my best short black skirt with the crocodile spike-heel boots. What do you think?"

"Hair up or down?"

"Up would be best, wouldn't it?"

"Absolutely."

"And then my one-carat emerald earrings."

"Wow! I didn't know you had those."

"I don't, but my birthday's coming, darling." She peeled off her shirt. "Could she have killed Barlow?"

"There's the question. Cody thinks not, but I think she could have. Practically the first thing she said to us was that Barlow deserved to die, and she'd thought about killing him."

"And you're thinking that she would only say

that to disarm you and throw you off the scent. Most innocent people would never imagine they might be a suspect, much less volunteer the idea before you asked. Am I right?"

"Perfectly. I thought she meant by that to tell us she didn't do it before we'd thought of it. You know what a contrarian I can be. Anyway, Denny Frost will probably be at the cocktail party. You can size her up yourself."

"I believe I will."

"As always." I already knew that Maya was ready to flirt with almost anyone, but it looked like she was about to prove it once again.

The cocktail party was staged like a film set on the extensive rooftop gardens of a bed and breakfast resting on the precipitous slopes of the Atascadero neighborhood. There, on a clear day, the views seemed to penetrate into northern Guatemala. The name of this hostelry was familiar to me, but I'd never been there before, although I'd seen this view from other places. Coming in, our names were checked off on a master list by the conference security maven, Lola Barker. She regarded us as if she had seen us before, possibly in a police lineup or a wanted poster, but without recalling when or where, and we may still just possibly have been trying to sneak in without paying. I began to wonder whether the world was really in a state of constant conspiracy trying to crash these conference events. I guess you never knew when some harmless-looking group could turn into a lethal threat. Not that Cody ever looked harmless, but that was more his style than Maya's and mine.

Inside the great room, once we'd been cleared, we drifted out onto a long terrace lined with servers bearing trays of canapés and short plastic glasses of red and white wine. In spite of the face-saving backstage maneuverings of Chad Metcalf, or perhaps because of them, the public façade of the conference still looked fairly convincing at this point. I reminded myself that the Zacher Agency was part of the presentation, but not the truth. Once the truth emerged, if it ever did, we were finished with our job.

Although I'd seen her face on the back of her book jackets, I was not prepared for the surprising scale of Dr. Ruth Bendickson. I'm a tiny fraction over six feet tall myself, passing it by about the thickness of a sock, but Dr. Ruth had to be at least six-foot-three, and she was wearing flats, which was the second thing I'd looked at. She could have stood opposite Cody and looked him directly in the eye. The pair of high-waisted black linen slacks she was wearing only emphasized the length of her legs. I suppose there was no point in trying to conceal it. Above the slacks she wore a white blouse with a ruffle collar and cuffs. She had no jewelry on her wrists or neck, and I couldn't get close enough to make out her rings. Her pixyish haircut seemed a little frivolous on a woman of her size, and from the light shining through it from behind, the hair itself looked thin. Her voice was also too high and singsong to be a good fit for anyone on her scale. Her diction had a dash of British overtones in it, as if she'd lived there for several years, or attended college in the United Kingdom. Nonetheless, her overall presence was impressive. I estimated her age at mid-fifties. I couldn't imagine her as a teenager and less as a child.

We separated to scan the crowd, and I held back from joining the knot of people surrounding Ruth Bendickson. Not knowing her work, I would've had little to say even if I'd had an opening to say it. Plenty of other people were struggling to get her attention. Maya was one of them, but it wasn't her manner to thrust herself deeply into a knot of eager gringos. From the corner of my eye I noticed

Cody off to one side, already deep in conversation with Denny Frost. He was bent over her like a crow descending on some delicate morsel of road kill. She was dressed in a lustrous mauve dress that emphasized her slender figure. The way it draped suggested silk, and it made her look almost frail. Was that the desired effect? Even frail people could deliver a fatal dose of poison—in fact, frailty could be an excellent cover.

Many faces in the crowd belonged to local people who were known to me: perhaps as many as one in five. Most of them would have been attending as readers and fans, rather than writers, and admission to this cocktail party could be obtained as a separate ticket. A person of Ruth Bendickson's literary stature was a strong draw, and there were easily more than 200 people in attendance. I plucked a glass of red wine off a passing server's tray and worked my way through the crowd, whose mood did not appear to be dampened by the death of Justus Barlow. Occasionally I caught his name.

Ahead I spotted Chad Metcalf, wearing a dark suit and tie, and speaking with two women. There weren't many other suits in view. At this point, I didn't have anything more to say to him. San Miguel is not a formal place, even on an occasion such as this. At a touch on my elbow, I turned to see Cody standing next to me looking a little uncomfortable. I had seen him in a jacket perhaps twice in eight years. It was the same blazer.

"What did Miss Denny have to add just now?" I said.

"I asked her about Amy Wendt and watched her reaction for clues."

"And?"

"Nothing. Not a blink. She just shook her head with a kind of serene smile."

"Of course, Amy Wendt's death was far enough back that she might never have heard of it. Barlow certainly would never have brought it up to her or any of his clients."

"Look at her now." Cody pointed with his glass. Miss Denny was standing next to Maya at the fringe of the Ruth Bendickson circle of admirers. The two were deep in conversation, the only ones not focused on the best selling mystery writer.

"That's good," I said. "Maya will give us a third opinion. She'll probably pry more out of Denny than we were able to."

"I wonder what it'll cost her," said Cody thoughtfully.

I shrugged. "I told Maya about our meeting,

so she knows what to expect. Besides, other women have hit on Maya in the past. She's fine with it. As she explained to me, the flirting style between two women is actually not that different. It's like going from Spanish to Portuguese, mostly a matter of a different emphasis and inflection. Yet it turns out that most of the verbs are quite similar." Cody looked at me as if he was almost convinced I knew what I was talking about.

As I watched, I could see from Maya's body language that she was on duty. After all, she was the head of the agency for good reason. Cody and I separated to look for our other suspects. Over the carved stone balustrade, the city lights carpeted the meandering hills with gems. I could see other parties in progress here and there. Through the next block a trio of arched windows displayed a party with a grand piano in play. Women in long dresses drifted out onto the terrace where uniformed waiters waited with trays. On the night air, I could hear the faraway sound of the music. I moved back into the crowd.

Dina Bauer was a woman of medium height who wore her thick dark hair in a chin-length bob. The subtle lights came off it quite well, giving me the sense that it was extremely clean. I had spotted her name on her conference badge soon after Cody moved off. I had wanted to see her there, and I'd circled the crowd a couple of times earlier, just to get a sense of her. I estimated her age at forty-five. She wasn't using much makeup, and overall, wore a serious expression, with a pair of slight vertical lines dividing her forehead into halves with a shallow ridge between. She looked as if this cocktail party were a research project she needed to take seriously as an assignment. Dina was dressed in a reddish-brown safari dress with a necklace of chunky amber beads. In a showy crowd like this she could easily have been overlooked, but she clearly wasn't working at being noticed. Before I approached, I studied her for a while longer, since I hadn't thought initially to do a full interview at the cocktail party. But why not, if she was alone? She might welcome a little interaction, and after a drink or two, she might be relaxed enough to talk at length about her Justus Barlow experience.

She was hanging back from the crowd that attended Ruth Bendickson's every word, watching the interaction. The author was seated in a tall, throne-like wicker chair. Dina Bauer's manner was hesitant, even a bit withdrawn, and I didn't see her interact with anyone while I watched her. I was glad Cody and Maya were both gone, because I didn't want to swarm her. Moving off in her direction, I thought I'd start by saying something about our keynote speaker and her work. It would be a fabrication, but Maya had fed me a few plausible lines for just this situation. I stopped at Dina's side and gave her a smile. She was swaying slightly, as if in time to a song that could only be heard inside her own head.

"I know who you are," she said, in a matter-of-fact tone, before I could begin. "You're Paul Zacher. I saw your photo in the brochure, and I'm planning to attend your agency's talk tomorrow."

"I'm flattered," I said. This looked like it could be easier than I'd expected. "Do you ever use detective agencies in your books?"

"Sometimes in passing. I'd use them more if I knew in better detail how they worked on a case." She looked as if she expected me to tell her.

"I'm working now. Please don't repeat this, but we're looking into the death of Justus Barlow. I know from his records that you were using his services on a book called *Less Than Zero*. Not bad on short notice, right?"

She gave me a level look. "I'm not surprised. I didn't go to hear his speech because I'd already had more than enough of him, and I'd also had more than enough of his views about adverbs. But someone told me that you were there. You saw him die, and you and your tall friend took charge of the room." There was no emotion in her voice. I couldn't read whether or not she was disappointed she wasn't there to see it happen herself.

"Yes, we were there. I wonder if you'd be willing to talk about your experience with him working on your manuscript? Of course, what you say would be confidential."

Dina Bauer placed her left arm across her chest, holding her wine glass in the other hand. She was looking at something across the terrace, but not at Ruth Bendickson.

"Let's start by saying I didn't find him sympathetic to what I was doing. You have to be on the same page to make that kind of interaction work, no pun intended." Her lips were thin and her expression unemotional. "Perhaps I wasn't his easiest client, because I have a peculiar way of coming at a story, and early on it was clear that he didn't agree with it."

"Can you explain that a bit more?"

She turned to face me. "I'm not a person who's in love with everyday reality. It's not that I can't handle it in my own life, which is going fine, by the way." She gave me a look that invited no intervention. "But I seem to be driven toward abnormal or paranormal events in my fiction. I'm not sure why, but I've come to accept it as my comfort zone. Maybe because it widens the playing field and allows me the latitude to bring in things that wouldn't happen to most people. It's a way of enhancing the plot. Do you think that's strange?"

"Are you talking about *spooky* things?" I couldn't think what else to call them. Aside from one case, our sixth, that we called *Vanishing Act* in our final report, we'd never encountered another situation even half that strange. She shrugged.

"Spooky is not my kind of term. My instincts are darker than that. Let me just say that if I used a ghost, it wouldn't be friendly and I wouldn't call him Caspar." Dina didn't say what term she did use in place of spooky. We were silent for a while, listening to the eager background babble around Ruth Bendickson, but without being able to make any of the words out clearly.

"When the unusual appears in my work," she went on, "I don't try to explain or rationalize it. I never prepare the reader for its sudden arrival. It's simply there, part of the story like anything else, as if the reader ought to be expecting it on her own."

I thought this sounded like a reasonable position, and it reminded me of the kind of uncompromising approach I often took as a painter. I thought of it as take it or leave it—it is what it is.

"How did you get started with Justus Barlow?"

"I was at the conference last year. This is my third time, actually. I had asked some questions at a panel discussion that were related to my use of paranormal occurrences, and Chad Metcalf approached me afterward and gave me Barlow's card. He said that was the kind of thing he could easily help with. It turned out that wasn't really the case, but by that time I'd already started with Barlow and he was giving me some other suggestions that were valuable." She frowned suddenly. "Well, at least useful."

"What's your current book about," I asked, "if you don't mind telling me? I know some writers don't like to talk about a work in progress." Dina Bauer was so self-possessed and almost abstract that I didn't feel I was getting much from her, aside from her simple, direct answers. Yet, she didn't seem at all evasive, something I was always sensitive to. Had she been touching me a lot, as some Méxican women like to do in a conversation, I would have been more comfortable, but most American women don't do that.

"It's about a Catholic priest who's looking into the death of a friend of his, and he discovers it may have had a supernatural element, although not one provided for in church doctrine or lore. He finds this disturbing, but he continues anyway. The closer he gets to an answer, the more his faith is challenged, even undermined. In the end, he practically has to renounce his beliefs as a priest to accept the logic of the crime. It's a devastating moment."

"Why do I think that he dies in the end?"

"You'll just have to read it when it comes out. As a detective yourself, I'd be interested in your take on it." For the first time she gave me a modest smile.

"I like the symmetry of that idea. The priest is forced to exchange one kind of belief for another in a way he never anticipated. He's used to being a man of faith, but in that case, one faith contradicts the other. Art can be uncomfortable, whether it's painting or writing." She gave me a brief smile again.

"I think you're getting it. Justus Barlow didn't like it, though. He said it operated on too many levels, and tried to do too many tasks, none of them well. 'Keep it simpler,' he said, 'otherwise you're going to move beyond your capabilities, and they're not that strong.'"

I was surprised that she'd tell me this so bluntly. "How did that make you feel?"

"Exactly the way he intended it to make me

feel. I had to ask myself again if I was really capable of pulling it off. It was a question I'd already considered earlier in the book. But after that initial reaction, I didn't believe him for a minute. I felt it was more a matter that the terrain I was operating in made him uncomfortable, even as it gave me room to stretch. That was the beginning of the decline in our relationship. Barlow could never stretch. He operated within a confined field, and he didn't try to climb over the self-imposed wall that enclosed him. He needed certainty, so my kind of serendipity scared the hell out of him. To me, he always advocated working from an outline and never deviating from it. In spite of how aggressive he behaved toward me individually, I felt that at bottom, he was a timid man. He barked the way a frightened dog does, it was all bluster. Life had burned him in some way—but he would never let you know how."

I found myself liking her insights. My impression had been that his short stature and his bad leg may have united to make him search for his fulfillment in authority and expertise. "Maybe that's why he was so aggressive toward you. I agree with you that aggressive façades are often caused by fear. Were you with him long enough to develop a sense of what your book would've been like if you'd followed his advice?"

"That really didn't take long. It would have had no humor, no paranormal elements, and certainly no hyperbole. The plot would've been dull and predictable. The priest would've solved the murder with no challenge to his belief system. How boring would that have been? I wanted the solution to come at considerable cost to the priest, and I wanted the possibility of his copping out to remain an option until the final chapter. Barlow liked to yammer on about dramatic tension, but to me, the challenge to the priest's beliefs was the best possible source of tension in the book. Barlow could've fit his version of it into a standard box much more easily than the book I was writing. Maybe he was thinking it would be easier to sell that way, but I had no confidence in his concept. I think you write the book first, then you sell it, but not every writer operates that way. I could never do a book proposal, because that early on I can't be sure of where it's going. That's the same reason I don't do outlines. I trust myself to get it right without all that structure. I think that if you write from formulas you start to sound too much like other writers. That's one of the reasons I hated his rant about adverbs."

A server came by and refilled our glasses. Dina watched Ruth.

"Serendipity," I said, nodding. "I understand it well. It works in painting too, and I'm also a painter. Step twelve can compel you to go to step thirteen, but often neither of them were visible from step one. Did Barlow ever come on to you?" I liked changeups like this. Dina didn't twitch.

"You mean did he behave himself?"

"Yes." I decided her pale gray eyes were attractive, largely because of their frankness and intelligence, which I'd been unable to see from across the terrace earlier. I also liked the way she stood her ground and gave me straight answers. She had kept her balance throughout.

"I guess so. He was hardly a lady's man, though, was he? I never got the sense that he was interested in me in that way."

"Were you finished with the book when he died?" I had seen his tally of her hours at the end of Dina Bauer's last page in the notebook, but there was no indication that they were finished with their sessions. It stood at twenty-seven hours on the day before his fatal speech, which I calculated would have been just short of $2300, at $85 an hour.

"That was under discussion."

"How do you mean?"

"I told him not to go any farther, and to give

me the bill."

"How much was it?"

"He said it was about forty-five hundred dollars at that point. He needed to check the detail and add it up before he gave me a firm number."

"I see." I was startled at this, but I kept my voice neutral as she went on.

"I thought that amount was a joke, and that he was cribbing the hours. I said I wouldn't pay it. He replied that people paid him eight or ten thousand dollars all the time, and he wouldn't give me the manuscript back, which had all his detailed comments, until I settled him out in full. That's where it stood at the end—it was a standoff. We hadn't scheduled another conversation."

"Was not recovering that manuscript a big loss? I mean, if the two of you weren't going in the same direction, how valuable would his written notes be?"

"Well, yes and no. Conceptually, it didn't matter, since I'd never bought into the direction he thought the book should go in. But in the more detailed comments he quoted to me in our phone sessions, I could often see a lot of value. The problem was that to me, in total they were still never worth the kind of money he wanted to charge me. He thought it was all about his time, but I thought it was more about the value of his services. Now you're wondering if I thought he was a charlatan, right?"

I nodded.

"Although I considered that, I don't think so. Barlow wasn't a complete fake, yet he still wasn't what he pretended to be, either. My bottom line sense of him was this: even though his ideas were irrelevant at times, he did know some things, maybe more than a few things, about construction, timing, pace, points of grammar, even word choice. But at the end, he was never an architect of books." Here she made a series of broad gestures. "He had no larger vision that I could see, no grand scale to his view. In some passages, he could miss the direction I was taking entirely, but yet he would quibble about the precise meaning of a single minor word or two. The detail was more meaningful to him than the long view. I thought he was a good line editor at best, but a good one is not that common." She paused and took a thoughtful sip of her wine. "Then there was the constant rant about shortness. How tiresome was that?"

"What was that about? Do you think it was because *he* was short?"

"Indirectly. He couldn't tolerate a short character. When he encountered one, he thought it was about him, and he'd run on and on about it session after session, at his standard rate. I got angry with him one day. It was when we were still doing this by phone before the conference. I said, 'Do you think everything is about you? Because it isn't, and this character isn't, either. Get over it and let's move on.'"

"What did he say?"

"He was offended, and he said that he didn't think that at all, but he could still tell when a character was based on him."

"He didn't listen."

"No. I do have a short character in *Less Than Zero*, one of the police detectives. I needed this guy to be short because there's a scene where an object physically passes over his head, and it would have hit someone of normal height. But it had nothing to do with Barlow's stature. I thought, why the hell am I paying him $85 an hour to rant about being short? No matter what he said, none of it was ever about him except in his own mind."

"Was he nasty to you? By that I mean did you ever feel he was scoring points off you psychologically?"

Dina Bauer nodded slowly. "Often, but it didn't bother me. I had heard that one of his early clients killed herself, but maybe that was only a rumor. After this morning, though, there might be something in it that could have a link to his death. He was a little man who wanted very much to be a big man in his field, and in his own life. Maybe if I hadn't been close to him in age, he would have tried to sleep with me to bring me under his control. I felt he was still in transition, or hoped to be, trying to reach his own identity, while I already knew who I was. Not that I don't continue to change within myself, but evolution is part of my persona."

I wanted to shake her hand, but instead I asked, mimicking Cody's fish-eye stare, "Did you ever want to kill him?"

She shook her head without looking at me. "Justus Barlow was never worth it. If I ever wanted to kill someone, it would be a person of my own stature, an equal threat, which he never was. I would've settled for not having anything to do with him again. I guess that's what I got, in a way. He was the kind of person who made you want to undergo a ritual cleansing treatment after you'd finished with him. A sweat lodge, something like that, where in the steam you could beat your bare back with birch branches to prepare for moving on."

"I could see that as a line in your book. I wonder if you got your title from your experience with

Barlow?"

"*Less Than Zero*? No, that's the last line of the book itself. But since you ask, I could have. Well, not really. That's not fair to him. Like a lot of people, Barlow was a mixed bag. His problem was that, unlike most of us, he would never have acknowledged that. He wasn't different from us, only superior to us in his own mind."

I didn't want to suggest that I thought her title had been used before. It didn't matter.

"I think that's what brought him down," I said. I thanked Dina Bauer and moved off toward Cody and Maya, who were standing by the carved stone balustrade at the far end of the terrace. Every eight feet or so, the run of columns was punctuated by an urn full of vermillion bougainvillea, a color that went well with buff limestone. I felt Dina was looking after me speculatively, but I didn't turn around. Had she handled me like she had apparently handled Barlow? I couldn't say; nothing she'd said had a false note to it, nor a condescending tone, at least to my ear. She had read him well. I'd found her surprisingly self-possessed, with an integrated sense of her own experience that seemed mature and insightful. I didn't come away with the feeling that she'd ever needed to kill Barlow. It was more like she would've elbowed him aside once he became too tiresome to bear. As she suggested, a permanent separation and a ritual bath would have served her needs just as well. It seemed like a good fit.

I was now thinking that the killer was a person who'd been more vulnerable to him than Dina Bauer had been, but in what way wasn't clear yet.

I paused at the edge of the Ruth Bendickson crowd, which hadn't diminished in size or enthusiasm. Maya and Cody joined me. Some fans had copies of Ruth's books under their arms, awaiting an autograph. Saying a sentence or two to each of them as they came up, she at least looked accommodating, if not quite welcoming. With three back-to-back best sellers, how many bookstore signings had she done? The Boston to New York corridor where she lived was full of them. I tried to imagine a world where people came up to me repeatedly and greeted me by name, yet I never recognized any of them. "Paul, you don't know me, but…" they would say. I suppose you can get used to anything. I preferred anonymity; I rarely carried my cell phone because I didn't care to be that available.

"Miss Denny's a big fan of Maya," Cody said.

"I'm thinking of changing sides," she

revealed with a mocking smile.

"Use it," I said, still mulling over my chat with Dina Bauer. "Use it like you do with men. Did you get into the case with her?"

"She only talked about her coming of age process. It was interesting, but it didn't have much bearing on the case. I like her; she has a different take on women. Although I also have some insights I'll share later when we're out of this crowd."

"I like her too, and Cody's ready to join the Confederate Army to court her, if that's what it takes, right Colonel?"

He didn't respond to this.

The crowd around us buzzed with book talk, and this close, I could make out individual snippets. Apparently, there was more to writing than I'd ever imagined, going way beyond rigid adverb avoidance. Painting is complicated too, but since it comes from the right side of the brain, many aspects of it have no words to describe them, so it can be harder to talk about in a group, or anywhere. Writing, coming from the left side, where all the words are stacked up in rows and ready to use, is brimming with ways to characterize the process. From what I was hearing, maybe there were too many available. Barlow had been trying to whittle the pile down to size. I suspected that in the end, writing all came down to a creative mind and a keyboard—similar to painting, except that you used a vase full of brushes and a pallet. They're both solitary tasks, where your most serious competition is what you achieved yesterday.

We circulated for a while, but, among the three of us, only Maya could be glib about books. Cody was rarely glib about anything other than evidence, except approaching Super Bowls, and I was mainly glib with a brush. The wine was not as good as we drank at home, and the canapés were sparse, with a preponderance of limp raw vegetables and dip that night have come on large plastic trays from the Mega Market. I could never handle vegetables, dip and a glass of wine simultaneously, so I just drank wine.

The setting was spectacular, with San Miguel laid out at our feet and all around on the slopes, yet, aside from the great natural view, the conference gathering conveyed the feeling of having been done on a strict budget, as if the stellar Ruth Bendickson, by all accounts the real deal, was being displayed on a cardboard stage set done in spray paint and sparkles. We'd already decided we had to talk to her about her time with Justus Barlow, but this wasn't the occasion. Chad Metcalf was still working the crowd, giving no impression that he had any idea who we were. He didn't glance our way once, and I gave him credit for that. I made several passes through the crowd, but I saw no nametag belonging to Lisa Givens, our final Barlow client suspect. At about 8:30 we slipped away to go down to Harry's (now called Hank's) to compare notes and relax with some real food and a martini you'd notice as it went down. As we walked out the door onto Calle Fuentes, I wondered whether the killer's eyes were on our backs. We were all silent and reflective until we got inside the van.

"Did that feel cheap to anyone besides me?" Cody asked as I drove down the sharply winding cobblestone slope toward Santo Domingo. If the cobblestones were wet, you might get to the bottom faster than you meant to. "For one thing, there weren't any shrimp, not even the little ones. I've been in classier places than that in Peoria."

"Just remember," I said, "we didn't have to pay to get in."

"Miss Denny told me the use of the terrace was donated by the bed and breakfast," said Maya. "I felt like the cost for each guest was calculated to the last centavo. In México we don't do it that way." For Maya, who grew up in México City, that was the meaning of *México*; it only referred to the capital. The rest of us lived in fly-over land. Our state of Guanajuato could have been Iowa.

"Maybe that's only careful management," I said, as we passed la Puertacita Hotel. I couldn't help but recall that James Watt had been murdered in one of their townhouses on our third case. "Metcalf has probably put on this event at least half a dozen times. If he hadn't figured how to make the numbers work by now, he would've already gone on to something more lucrative."

"Now that makes me wonder if the conference benefits from Barlow's death?" Cody said.

Maya turned around in the passenger seat to look at him. "Which is saying that Chad Metcalf benefits, because he is everything. How would that happen?"

"What if it's like making a movie or doing a theater production? You can buy insurance that guarantees the stars are alive and well enough to work when the cameras start rolling or the curtain goes up. And you can't insure someone's life without their signature; they would have to know about it."

"Then we should ask Ruth Bendickson if she was insured when we talk to her," said Maya. "Because if Justus Barlow was insured, then she has even more reason to be."

CHAPTER SIX

At ten o'clock on the morning of the second day of the conference, the entire staff of the Paul Zacher Agency assembled in one of several open conference rooms on the lower floor of the Rosewood. Seated behind an eight-foot table with a starched white tablecloth displaying a pitcher and three water glasses, we faced a crowd that had taken up all fifty seats. Four or five people stood along the wall at the back. I hadn't thought we would fill the room. The title of our session was, *Real Detectives at Work*. No one was laughing, yet. I was already hoping that this meeting was not going to turn out to be about us.

Cody was to begin, speaking on the methodology of taking on a case, starting with data gathering and the intake interview. He was wearing the same navy blazer that he couldn't have buttoned in front even if it had been bulletproof, and a pair of khaki pants I'd never seen on him before. They looked new, as if he'd run up to the Liverpool department store and bought them just for this event. As it was explained to us by Metcalf's session presenter liaison, the point of our conference participation was to lend some anchoring reality to writers who wanted to use detective agencies in their books in a supporting role. I didn't know how typical we would be, but Maya had told us that for what little support the conference was offering, no other agency had been willing to come down to San Miguel and give a presentation about their process. It paid nothing more than the freedom to attend the other conference sessions for nothing and sell our books in the improvised bookstore. Among us, the only one with a book to sell was Maya, and she had brought a few copies of her volume about the early days of our town hero and revolutionary founding father, Ignacio Allende, published both in Spanish and English. Hopefully, she'd bought a fountain pen at Office Depot to autograph copies, but I hadn't seen it.

Coming in, Chad Metcalf nodded in acknowledgement to the crowd before he bent over our table confidentially. "Try to keep their questions off the Barlow situation," he whispered with a raise of his eyebrows. "I've had way too much of that already. Make no reference to working for the conference, either." We smiled back at him, but this was already our policy. I had already coached Maya on the word *glib*, in case she didn't already know it, so she knew what Chad was up to. We never talk publicly about cases in progress.

As Metcalf started his introduction, I glanced over at Cody. He was scanning his notes, and the papers in his hands displayed a slight tremor. I was a little nervous myself. We all knew our assigned material well enough, but delivering it smoothly in this venue was new and chancy. I had no experience speaking to a group like this, or any group for that matter. Maya had done a few presentations for her book, one to the San Miguel Rotary Club, so she may have been more relaxed as a speaker. With her great looks and nearly perfect English, she always got an enthusiastic reception. She was going to talk about agency management, including police relations—which were critical—while after that I planned to address the benefits of seeing things differently, which as an artist, was a unique asset I brought to our efforts. It didn't always work, but it sounded good. I knew it was an angle this crowd wouldn't expect.

"...often insightful and downright courageous," Metcalf was saying. "Because of its natural policy of discretion, the activities of the Paul Zacher Agency have not been well publicized in San Miguel, and may never be, yet what they bring to this conference is an insider's view of process and procedure like none other."

Metcalf had asked us for two paragraphs of background information to use in this introduction, and Maya had willingly generated some convincing boilerplate for him, a text we could almost have put in our next brochure. He had taken her suggestions like a press release, delivering the material word for word. Especially since the death of Justus Barlow, Metcalf had too many other things to think about anyway, and we were small potatoes next to the upscale literary heroes in attendance. At least he had the ability to make reading from a four by six index card sound like relatively spontaneous speech. I was facing his back, looking at his elbows pumping as he spoke, and the way his maroon sport coat divided at the top of his muscular buttocks. I was sure that on the other side of that picture, the lights glinted winningly off his perfectly bleached teeth. Next to me, seated at the center of the table, Maya beamed as he quoted her like the Delphic oracle.

"Therefore, to begin, I would like to present retired homicide detective Cody Williams, speaking on the critical value of correct procedure as step one. Cody?" Chad initiated the mild applause that followed, and the crowd looked genuinely curious.

All eyes were on him while Cody rose unsteadily as if trying to stabilize his footing on a slippery bed of rotted garbage. The fact that he had killed four men wouldn't help him here.

"Thank you, Chad," he began, taking a deep breath. With his reading glasses far down his nose, he regarded the notes in his hand for a moment with a wrinkled brow. Over the heads of the crowd, I could see that Chad Metcalf was already slipping out the door at the back of the room. Cody looked up and focused on someone in the fifth row. That, he'd explained to me earlier, was his strategy to connect with the audience, one at a time.

"The first few moments of a detective's entry on a crime scene are the most critical in the case, and all his powers of observation are called into play. This is when the scene is freshest, and it will only deteriorate from there as a reliable source of information." He glanced up at the crowd as if expecting a challenge, but none materialized. "As a writer describing this scene, this is also your chance to introduce or withhold information from your reader, depending on what the needs of your plot are. But if you withhold information, you run the risk of making your detective character seem unobservant, or not as intelligent as you want him to look, especially at the end when he solves the crime. Unobservant equates here to incompetent, so a balanced approach is in order."

I could now see a faint cluster of sweaty droplets blooming on his upper lip. Cody was already earning his money, not that there was any.

"When I enter a crime scene, and bear in mind that I practiced this for thirty years on the force in Illinois, and a handful more in the Zacher Agency here in San Miguel, the first thing I examine is…"

In mid phrase Cody was interrupted by a woman wildly waving her arms in the front row, sitting so close that he couldn't ignore her. He frowned. "If you don't mind, I'd like to take any questions at the end."

"Was Justus Barlow's death yesterday a murder?" she yelled from five feet away, ignoring his request. "I saw you talking to Denny Frost, and I know she was using him on her book. Do you think she killed him?" Five other hands went up behind her. A buzz of rapid conversation broke out in three or four places within the group. I heard Denny's name repeated several times. Cody looked exasperated. I noticed Dina Bauer seated toward the back, shaking her head at the disruption. A woman in the third row stood up.

"Has the Zacher Agency already been hired to take this case? And if not, why not? You're already here. As they say on TV, you guys were in place when it happened."

"I'm not able to comment on that at this time." Cody was now acting like he was responding to a reporter's question, something he must have had years of experience with. Several more people stood up and raised their hands.

"Do you have any other suspects?" someone shouted without waiting to be called on.

"I think you can't comment because it's an ongoing investigation, isn't that right?" yelled a man in back. "That's procedure, isn't it? We're talking about procedure already."

"If you ask me, I think you *won't* comment. I'll bet you could if you wanted to. Procedure be damned! Let's have the facts here! People always hide behind procedure. What are *you* hiding? We paid good money for this! Let's hear it!"

"Yeah, all of it!"

Cody was merely glancing from one outburst to another. Finally he raised both hands. "If I could please have your attention!"

"*You're* not the head of the Paul Zacher Agency anyway—I heard that she is." A man pointed rudely at Maya. She stood up with her hands outstretched and tried to respond, but was shouted down by three people who were also shouting each other down.

"And I heard that Justus Barlow deserved what he got. Someone said he was a creep. Is that true? Probably no jury would ever convict his killer."

"It's like O J Simpson all over again. Remember that one?"

"Do you think Ruth Bendickson is in any danger? Shouldn't she have some protection if there's a killer loose?"

"What great material! I can use all of this in my book. Now I know how it ends!"

At the back of the room, the door flew open and half a dozen more people rushed in and started pushing toward the front. The aisles were now full of people who had left their seats and begun milling around. Anyone still seated couldn't see anything except the backs of people standing in front of them.

"Who are these people coming in? Don't we need more security here?" a woman shouted. "My neighbor told me this would happen if I went to

México."

"Mine too. I'm scared to walk down the streets here, even in daylight. I *never* take my purse anywhere."

At this, Cody looked at us with a blank expression. Although we hadn't moved from our seats, we now found ourselves in the middle of the crowd, which had surged forward to surround our table. More people had entered from the back as the corridor was emptying into our meeting. All the aisles were blocked with arguing people.

"Let's have a progress report on the Barlow case!" one man started shouting. "This concerns all of us!" Several others began repeating in a chant, "This concerns all of us!" I felt like we were witnessing the birth of the Occupy the International Mystery Writers' Conference movement.

"Every one of us is at risk!"

Out of nowhere a voice between a shriek and a bellow ripped through the confusion.

"Shut up and sit down this instant! Take your seats!"

Like a zipper opening in taut fabric, the crowd in the center aisle parted in surprise to reveal Lola Barker standing at the rear of the room, her fists knotted on her hips. "*Do it now!*" she roared again, advancing to the front edge of our table and turning around, where she waited for silence. "The capacity of this room is fifty-five people. Anyone who was not here when Chad Metcalf introduced the speakers must LEAVE THIS INSTANT!" She urged them toward the back with her arms as if herding them out, but for a brief moment, no one moved. The room fell deadly silent. Lola Barker seemed to swell in both size and threat. Her voluminous chest was heaving. Here was the tipping point.

"All right then, get the hell out! Every goddamned one of you! Go! Clear the room now!"

I couldn't see her face, but it must have been livid. I hadn't realized she was Chad Metcalf's personal storm trooper. He could keep his razor-cut silver mane flawless while Lola, with her voice like a jackhammer, indiscriminately clubbed people into submission. Two women half way down the main aisle buckled and turned to leave, and as if the keystone had been yanked from the arch, the entire crowd crumbled after them, pushing and tripping, until in less than two minutes, the room was empty except for the four of us at the front. With a triumphant smirk over her left shoulder in Maya's direction, Lola Barker followed them out and slammed the door behind her, leaving us alone.

The sound rang in the air as we sat there stunned. With my mouth open, I looked back and forth at Maya and Cody.

"I didn't think we needed riot gear," he said. "We'll know better what to bring next time we do one of these."

"Did you ever have any training in crowd control?" I asked.

"Not enough, apparently. I guess I could use a lesson from Lola Barker. Even without a police baton, she's a master."

Still stunned, with a dazed look, Maya picked up a folded scrap of paper from the corner of the table and opened it. It hadn't been there when we started. She read it and passed it to me. On it in block capitals were written four words: LOOK AT AMY WENDT. Maya shrugged. "Does that mean anything to you?"

When I briefed Maya the afternoon before, I hadn't mentioned Amy Wendt, because at more than five years back, her death didn't seem current enough to be part of the case. I gave the paper to Cody. "Yes it does, but she's been dead for years. I don't see any connection, unless she's returned as a ghost." I told her what we'd seen in Barlow's notebook. "Did you happen to notice who dropped that note on the table?"

"No. It was all too chaotic."

"I think that was the point. Anyone in this room could've left it."

"Thank God for the occasional anonymous tip," Cody said. "We can dig into this easily since we've got Amy Wendt's contact information from the notebook. Even after five years, it might still connect us with a family member."

"Doesn't it seem like it was left by someone who thought we'd know who Amy Wendt was?" I said.

"Absolutely," he continued, "and at least we can get some idea how she died, too. The county of her residence would have her death certificate. It's always in the public record." He pulled out his cell and punched in a number. I assumed he was reaching his friends in the Chicago Police Department. From Barlow's notebook I remembered that Amy Wendt had been an instructor at Briarcliffe College on Long Island, and the Chicago cops would be able to get the death certificate from whatever county that was located in, and do it far faster than we could from San Miguel.

"I guess we've been cancelled," said Maya with obvious disappointment in her voice. I knew the rudeness of the crowd was beyond her range of expectations. Méxicans are normally too polite to behave like that. Part of it may also have been Lola Barker's startling persona, which was beyond any identifiable race or gender.

"We were popular, though, if a little controversial." I turned to Maya. "I heard someone in the corridor say that controversy can sell books, even when it's not all good." Cody went off in the corner to have his phone conversation. Going out the door a few minutes later, we found the crowd had mostly dispersed as we walked back toward the stairway. When we reached the conference bookstore at the end of the hall, we were confronted by Lola Barker again, breathing hard.

"The Director has asked me to collect your attendance badges," she said brightly.

"Why is that?"

"Well, you didn't give your presentation, did you? I guess that's clear enough." She raised her wrist and tapped the face of her watch. "You were barely in there for ten minutes, not eighty—you didn't produce, and worse yet, you had to be *rescued*. That doesn't meet our conference standard for presenters, not by a long shot." Her smug tone suggested she was speaking to guilty children.

"Was that our fault?" I said. I didn't care much myself, but I knew Maya would miss it. The right to attend the other presentations was our only compensation for what we'd been through. Looking at the brochure, we'd noticed that Metcalf was even selling individual tickets to some of them for between $60 and $80. I wondered what he might have gotten for ours, and would he now be issuing refunds? The loss of that income was probably what had angered him, so I could see why he'd asked Lola to yank our credentials. She must have called him right after she left our meeting room.

"You could hardly think it's the fault of the conference, since it was you who lost control of the crowd, wasn't it? It takes a certain level of *skill* to do these things. You'd think that with three of you, one of you could've come up with it. Maybe you weren't sufficiently prepared. If you ever do this again, show them some backbone if they get rowdy. Don't cut 'em any slack. You guys lost it in there. There's just no excuse for that, OK? We try to avoid using amateurs here. If this wasn't such a hick town, there would've been another detective agency. I can see how you guys survive here—there's no competition."

Stunned into silence, we pulled off our badges and gave them to her. The looks on our faces must have conveyed something nasty, because she threw up her hands as if she were the injured party.

"Hey, don't blame me, people, I'm just the messenger here. I'm a poor, unpaid volunteer, and I can only do what I'm told." She stalked off with a light-hearted swing to her hips and our badges twirling in her hand.

"She was only following orders," said Cody, staring after her. "And I think the unpaid part is bullshit."

"At least my books are still for sale," said Maya. "That's something." We walked back to her table in the bookstore to see if she'd sold any, but found it empty. Had she sold them all? Evidently we hadn't brought enough. So who knew this would be her target market? They were probably scooping up anything about México. When we stopped to ask the cashier if she needed more, we noticed Maya's six books in a box at her feet. Maya's face dropped.

"Why not take these with you on your way out?" the cashier said. "Selling books here is a privilege restricted to paid conference participants and presenters. It's not for the general public." We didn't wait for her to add that she was only doing what she'd been told.

Two hours later we assembled at la Posadita for lunch. It's a rooftop place on Cuna de Allende, across from the long side of the Parroquia, the big church fronting the plaza. There, from a dozen or so tables under sun umbrellas, people can admire a view toward the hilly environs in the southwestern part of town. The terraces of neighboring roof gardens bloom with palms and ficus trees, and in some places, stands of Italian cypress punctuate the blazing sky with their needle-like forms. They provide emphasis to the calendar-quality scenery. Everywhere, vibrant shades of bougainvillea, from pale pink to flaming scarlet and apricot, spill over the ramparts. The main reason to come there for lunch, although unspoken among us, was that it was friendly, familiar, and it offered cover for an agency staff that had been poorly used, and for no good reason that we could see.

"That was a tough crowd," Cody said as he removed his blazer and draped it over one of those little wrought iron stands at tableside that holds your purse, or your ego to keep it from being stomped on again by uncaring passersby.

"I feel like we stepped in front of a bus," Maya said.

The service there is attentive, and the pulled pork excellent. I never look at the menu. Maya unrolled her napkin and set the silverware aside. "What have we got?" she said to Cody. "Is Chicago still doing your errands?" He had carefully maintained his relations with his former associates in the Chicago Police Department. It had already paid off for us more than a dozen times as a quick source of information we couldn't otherwise get.

"Of course." Cody pulled out a notebook from his shirt pocket. "Here's what they came up with. Amy Wendt, age twenty-six at the time of her death a little more than five years ago."

"Cause of death?" I asked.

"Suicide by barbiturate overdose in combination with alcohol. That was from the death certificate."

"Did you reach the family?"

"The only surviving family member is her brother Michael, current age thirty-eight, who lives in their parents' house in Bethpage, Long island. They had inherited it jointly at their mother's death from cancer, a year and a half before Amy died. No mention made of the father, but apparently he's no longer in the picture."

The waiter came over and we ordered drinks.

Maya had lemonade with mineral water. Cody and I had Negra Modelos.

"Was Michael Wendt willing to talk about his sister's death at all?" asked Maya.

"He was when I told him we were investigating the death of Justus Barlow. The noise he made sounded like a triumphant snort. Michael Wendt called him a sour bastard and said he hoped it was murder, because then justice would be done. Without commenting on that, I said I knew Amy had worked with Barlow on two of her books. Do you know what his answer was?"

"No."

"He said, 'I wish I still had them now. From the passages Amy showed me, I thought they were great.' It turns out that Amy erased the computer files on both of them before she killed herself. He said she left nothing behind, not even her notes. Everything was gone."

"But couldn't they be recovered if he still has her computer?" Maya said.

"That was the second thing I asked. That's gone too. He donated it to a computer literacy project in the Bronx."

"What kind of person does what she did?" I said, wondering what it would be like to kill myself after first burning all my paintings. Maybe just doing something that stupid would make me want to kill myself. I couldn't imagine that anything else could. "Was it self-hatred, a desire to vacate the scene and leave no single trace of your prior existence? Particularly, to destroy the things that had been most important to you?" From the little we knew it looked like an obliteration of everything she valued, not only her life. Maybe those two books had displayed the same kind of bitterness.

Cody shrugged. "I only talked to him for about ten minutes, but from what I know of psychology, I'd say you're not far off. Michael Wendt said his sister was highly unstable, and had been from early adolescence. In college and after, she was very creative and original, but subject to deep slumps where she couldn't write, couldn't even do some of the basic things to keep her life together, like cook a meal or show up for work. Because of that, she had a poor employment history, of course, and had only been teaching freshman English at Briarcliffe for two months when she died. The brother called her a genius, although my assessment would be more on the order of undiagnosed bipolar disorder."

"How could no one diagnose it? She sounds flat out *loca*." Maya said.

"The person who has it often avoids all the professionals who might recognize it. When Amy was on the upside of the emotional curve, she wouldn't think there was any problem—she was on a roll. According to Michael, at those times she was damn good at whatever she did. But on the downside, she was often in bed with the curtains drawn, hiding from everything. She was subject to migraines and stomach disorders. That part resembles severe depression with complications."

"I'm beginning to see now how it must have gone," I said. "With that psychological makeup, Amy Wendt had the misfortune to end up connecting with Barlow as his client. With his abusive tendencies, it must have been like lighting a fuse to her condition, although she probably coped with him all right when she was on the up side."

"And get this," said Cody, pouring the rest of his beer into the glass. "Barlow was recommended to her by Chad Metcalf. Her brother said Amy met Chad when he was teaching a course in community activism at City College in Manhattan, where she was ultimately fired for not showing up to teach English."

"And Metcalf couldn't foresee what a terrible combination that would be?" asked Maya.

"Maybe he didn't know her well," he said.

"Or maybe Chad didn't know what a predator Barlow was," I suggested. "They might have only been friends. Chad isn't a writer, as far as I know. He's just an organizer, a producer of this event. Since he'd never used Barlow's book editing services, he might be completely ignorant of the way he operated with his clients."

The waiter returned, and we ordered lunch.

Half an hour later, we were about halfway through it, chatting about our chaotic reception at the breakout session, when Maya asked, "So why did someone leave that note on our table? It had to be a person who suspected we were investigating Barlow's death, or even knew about it, and thought Amy Wendt's suicide was part of it."

I had heard of the "dead hand," the phenomenon where the deceased, through a will with highly specific and ironclad provisions, seeks to control his assets for many years after his death. In this case Amy Wendt had done the opposite, and there was nothing left for her or anyone else to control. It was more like she wanted to be forgotten. Only Justus Barlow could have said what happened between them in detail, not that I would have trusted his account had he been around to give it. The comments in his notebook, cut short as they'd been by her death, were too scant to be revealing.

"I don't think this is any use to us," Maya said. "Amy Wendt kills herself. It's tragic and, unless there's more we don't know, it's obviously connected to Barlow, since she destroyed her books too. But it doesn't seem like she was going to have a long life anyway, wired the way she was. It's sad that her books are gone, but I don't know what help having them would be at this point. It's no more than another bad recommendation of Barlow's services, this time fatally bad."

Cody was nodding. "That's right. The situation contains no new information, except that Chad Metcalf was feeding Barlow more clients than we knew."

"What a good and loyal friend," I said. "Everyone else is just fodder for the Barlow abuse machine."

"And since Chad Metcalf never used Barlow himself, he's not responsible for what happened, because he can always plead ignorance," said Maya. "He was only trying to help out a friend by sending some business his way."

"Isn't that what friends are for?" Cody said.

CHAPTER SEVEN

Diego Delgado reached my cell phone just after three that afternoon. We went through the usual courteous dance that would typically precede the delivery of any set of autopsy results here.

"I'm glad your son is fine," I said. "I hope he does well in the coming exams."

"And Maya, she is well?"

"The same as always, thank you. She's growing her hair longer again."

"I can't wait to see it!" This I believed. He'd always been a huge fan of hers, especially since he'd seen some of the nudes I was doing of her several years ago.

It was usually at about this point that I ran out of gas on the exchange of courtesies. "Was it poison?"

"Probably, but none of the usual suspects.

153

Señor Barlow experienced an overdose of Digoxin, which I am told can easily be fatal. The prescription quantities are miniscule."

"I wondered if it wasn't that."

"So, it was you who was in his hotel room after his death?"

"Of course. We thought it was murder, but you weren't ready to commit. We wanted to examine the scene while it was still fresh. You know how evidence is. It goes off quicker than raw fish in the sun on a hot day in Chihuahua." There was a moment of silence as Delgado digested this.

"I understand, and I'm glad, because the room has already been cleaned for the next tenant since then, although his belongings are still there. I trust that you kept some souvenirs from your visit?"

"We have his client notebook. I'll get it copied for us and drop it off at your office. Did you come up with anything in his room?"

"More in his body than in his room. I am finding it extremely difficult to believe he overdosed accidentally. The excess amount of Digoxin in his blood was still several times a normal dose, and considering the half-life factor, to start with he must have taken eight or ten times what his prescription called for. That would have been much more than enough."

"What do you think?"

"I'll tell you while you buy me breakfast in the morning. Bring me the original of that notebook, if you would." I thought this was unusually direct for Delgado, but maybe he was smarting a little because we'd gotten out ahead of him on this case. We always had more latitude than he did about when to get involved.

Ten minutes later, I dropped Barlow's notebook off at Office Depot for copying, and spent a half hour wandering around La Luciérnaga Mall while I waited. Here you could also find a Radio Shack and a MacDonald's for those expats who wanted to forget where they were. Méxicans liked them because they suggested this town was part of the real world of the twenty-first century, rather than a dusty old watering hole from 1542, which is how I preferred to think of it. People come here for different reasons. Some of the Méxicans in this town tend to think the expats are all old and hung up on the past.

At ten o'clock the next morning I went down the hill and met Delgado for breakfast at Hecho en México, a dependably good dining spot on the Ancha de San Antonio, not far from the site of our recent murder. It's right around the corner from the

Rosewood, tucked into the northern end of the Instituto building. I was surprised to see Delgado already seated as I walked in. He rose, and we repeated our earlier greeting from the phone call with minor variations in phrasing. When we sat down, I slid Barlow's notebook across the table to him.

"The fact that you are paying for this without complaint suggests you now have a client on this case," he said. Delgado was the only person present wearing a suit, and he was getting a few looks. He stuck his finger in his collar and made a half a circuit with it. We were still in the first half of March, but the weather was already heating up. May is the hottest month here.

I gave him my best Méxican shrug which by now is nearly as good as any you could get from the locals down in the plaza, which is where I learned it. He waited for me to tell him who our client was, but I didn't. Confidentiality still means something to me.

"It can only be the conference itself, and that in the person of Señor Metcalf. As expert as you and your associates are, I don't think the Rosewood would hire you."

"Why not?" This took me by surprise, and I heard a note of indignation in my response that I hadn't intended to put there.

"They have their own security. They are from a big company in Gringolandia. We have already talked to them." It was his way of being ahead of us.

"What do they think?"

"They're waiting for the autopsy report—a sensible position."

The waiter brought a basket of *bolillos*. "Did you give it to them?"

"Not just yet. All in good time. As we say here, when we are ready, because there are bureaucratic niceties to be observed. Even though they have little respect for the law, Méxicans have always been orderly people. Events must have the proper sequence. After your long residence here, I assumed you understood this."

I immediately thought of Zapata and Pancho Villa, for whom order was their main concern. "I'm getting it, *poco a poco*." Little by little. I translated the sequence part to mean that he didn't care to be scooped by some smart-ass gringo out-of-towners blowing into San Miguel for a single case and showing up the local constabulary. He'd probably let them know the autopsy results only after the case was solved. They could credit him or not, but he wouldn't expect it. I ordered an artichoke heart omelet with a side of bacon. Delgado had the *arrachera*, a marinated skirt steak as tender as a maiden's heart. I thought this was a little heavy for breakfast, but he knew better than I did what it took to get him through the day.

"What did you find in here?" He tapped the notebook with his left hand as he buttered a *bolillo*.

"It's all about his clients, going back nearly seven years. I don't want to influence your take on it, but you'll find he was cynical in the way he treated them. You'll be reading a book full of motives for murder. All you'll need is means and opportunity. You saw those three manuscripts in his hotel room, so you know what clients he was seeing there toward the end. That's where we started, anyway. I don't want to tell you your job, because, as always, you are the expert."

His hand in midair, Delgado regarded me with a veiled look, as if I were intentionally impeding his investigation, something I did only when I needed to.

"*Three* manuscripts, do you say this?"

I nodded, getting an inkling of what was coming. I could pronounce *tres* as well as any Méxican. After all, it only had one R in it.

"And you took one of them away with you, then? Perhaps because it was of greater interest than the others? I can imagine you doing this."

"No, we left them all in a pile on the desk."

Delgado stopped chewing and nodded slowly. "Now I can see some additional benefit to your visit ahead of ours. We will know from this which manuscript we were not permitted to see. The next task becomes how to see it." He pulled a small notebook from his inner jacket pocket. "I have already the books from las Señoritas Dina Bauer and Denny Frost."

"Then you are missing the one from a *señorita* named Lisa Givens."

Delgado wrote this down. "With a B?"

"GiVens, with a V." This is often a source of confusion.

"Did you look at it?" His eyebrows lifted in an apparent attempt to unite with his hairline, which rested at no great distance above them.

"Only to take her name and page through it. Barlow's treatment of it was no different from the others. The pages had been roughly handled, full of stains and creases. I recall a pinfeather stuck to the top of page four like an exclamation point. The markings were all in blunt pencil, many of them illegible."

"Yet this Señor Barlow was a professional,

no? How could this be? He did not have the pride of his job?"

I thought Delgado's question was dead on, but explaining the mind of Justus Barlow was more a task for Cody, with his strong psychology background, than it was for me. I leaned forward over the table. "Señor Delgado, you are of the Policía Judicial. Your expertise is much bigger than mine in this area. Please recall that I am only an artist who sees things differently, and that's what I bring to my agency. To me, Barlow looks like a predator with a few valid credentials, but not the degree of skill he pretended to have. More than that, like why he acted as he did toward his clients, I don't know. The solution to this case, from what I've seen so far, lies among the experiences of his victims. As you suggest, the best clue so far, other than the residue of Digoxin in his blood, is the disappearance of the manuscript of Lisa Givens. You'll find Justus Barlow's critical comments about her work in the last three pages of this notebook, but I think you'll still want the manuscript itself."

"You have not talked to her?"

"No. I have her cell phone number here, but she hasn't responded to my calls." I pulled out my notes from the conference reception desk information and gave him Lisa's cell number, which he could also get from the notebook. Maybe her cell wasn't working here; I couldn't tell from the message I was getting when I dialed it. At that point, the waiter brought breakfast. Delgado asked me to characterize the conference. What kind of person, for example, he wanted to know, would attend such an event?

"First of all, people who need an excuse to get out of their winter climate for a week or ten days. The conference provides a business rationale for fun in the sun. Then there's a small group of working writers who are there mainly to promote their books by giving instruction in writing, marketing, and selling to an agent or publisher."

"And this is a big business?"

"The publishing part is, and from what I'm hearing, it's changing every day. The last and largest group attending are people who would like to be mystery writers, or writers of any kind, but for various reasons, they aren't yet."

"They are not really writing?"

"That's my take on it. They're what we call wannabes." I tried to find a good Spanish word for this, but failed.

"What do you think of Señor Metcalf?"

"He's slick, polished, and comfortable in the

world of event promotion. I don't think he knows the slightest thing about writing, and he operates with a small core of part-time paid help, and below that a body of volunteers who want to get in free and rub elbows with real writers. My guess is that he starts recruiting the volunteers in each new location five or six months before the conference. Maybe even before that."

Delgado chewed on this between bites of his *arrachera*. "So he will not be back to San Miguel. Each time it occurs in a different place, yes?"

I nodded with a grin.

He and I spent the rest of our visit talking about the upcoming presidential election in July. He felt that if the old **PRI** party returned to power, which appeared likely, they could once again make a profitable deal with the drug cartels, like they had in the old days, and the turf wars on the border would clear up. With a single official illegal drug wholesaler, business would be normal again, and the Americans, he felt certain, could buy their recreational drugs with more security. There would be peace in the valley, and everyone would feel just fine. Maybe then the American newspapers and TV could find a new subject to rant about and the tourists would come back. Business would be good once again.

Although I was surprised at his frankness, I found no reason to disagree.

Delgado and I parted at Codo and he walked back to his office on the plaza. I went up Zacateros toward home. There I found Maya studying the notebook copy, tapping the eraser end of her pencil on the tabletop. I sensed that she was a bit at loose ends, since we'd been ejected from the conference. Ruth Bendickson's keynote address was scheduled for this evening, and now we wouldn't be going. The individual tickets had been sold out. The subject of the talk was *The Mystery Within Ourselves*. That would have been a high point for Maya, and I thought it sounded promising myself.

"There's not much variety in this material," she said. "Barlow used the same technique to batter all of his clients. He found something in the manuscript that he felt didn't work and beat the drum about it until the writer caved in."

"I'm not surprised. He stayed with what he knew." I went on to tell her about the coroner finding a high level of Digoxin in Barlow's blood.

"So we were right."

"The prescribed dosage level on the bottle we saw in his bathroom was miniscule. He would have had to take something like eight or more tablets to

163

reach the level that was still in his blood at the time of the autopsy. Delgado's on the case now. I gave him the notebook."

"I thought that was why we have this copy."

"I want to look at Lisa Givens' profile again. I barely skimmed it before."

Maya passed me the notebook.

"Twenty-nine years old, lives in Laramie, Wyoming. Divorced with no children. Barlow always wants to know their marital status. Wait, this is interesting."

"What?"

"Lisa Givens was not an English major. She studied pharmacy at Case Western Reserve in Cleveland, a good school."

"I think this sounds like bingo," Maya said.

"And now she's writing mysteries, or trying to. I wonder what her favorite cause of death is? I'm beginning to understand now why her manuscript disappeared, and she's not returning my calls."

"We still have to talk to her. I'll call Cody and you two can cover all the rest of the sessions going on this afternoon until we find her. I'm not sure I'm ready to look at those people again."

CHAPTER EIGHT
CODY WILLIAMS

Breakout Session XII: The Plot Thickens, but Does the Thinner Plot Run Faster? This was the hand-printed legend on a placard pinned to a cork tablet next to the door of the first small meeting room next to the conference lobby. Cody didn't recognize the name of the presenter. The door itself was closed and locked, as he discovered when he tried to silently turn the knob and slip in to look for Lisa Givens. He listened for a moment, but beyond a subtle murmur of voices, he could make out nothing. On the short corridor where he stood, two other rooms were in session. He tried to think of alternatives to knocking. On a similar offshoot corridor down the hall, Paul was looking for Lisa too.

Cody was not a man to walk outside his condo door without carrying a few key resources. One was his gun, although this usually stayed at home when no dangerous case was in progress. The same was true of the handcuff pack hanging at the back of his belt, which often bothered his backbone as he sat at Harry's, yet he didn't feel he could set it on the table. His lock picks, housed in a smooth black pigskin case next to his wallet, and about the same thickness, were always available, but never visible.

He studied the knob for a moment. Finished in a brushed bronze surface, it was obviously a premium-level installation, but one he didn't recognize. It wasn't, he thought, made in the United States, although it might be European. More likely, it was from México City. But locks were locks, and the possible variations had already been explored centuries before. They were now about how much the owner wanted to spend on security, because more security meant more elaboration. Cody pulled out the pick case and opened it to extract the longest probe, one he called the stiletto. Sliding it millimeter by millimeter into the lock, he felt the device touch resistance at four subtle points. At this initial stage, picking a lock was all about information. The second stage was about turning over the tumblers one at a time. This one had four, each awaiting his practiced touch. Picking a lock like this made Cody feel almost Sicilian, and therefore, in his mind, dangerous. He had recently turned sixty, and he didn't mind being dangerous.

As he worked the probe around inside the lock, trying to make no noise, the knob suddenly turned in his hand. The door drew inward a few inches. In the space between it and the jamb, a vertical wedge of Lola Barker's puffy face appeared and the single visible eye regarded Cody with suspicion. He withdrew the pick and stuck it in his shirt pocket as he placed his other hand on the door. She tried to push it closed as he forced it open. From inside he could hear the speaker droning on about movement in plot. Inch by inch, Cody forced the door further ajar until it stood open more than ninety degrees.

"Go away!" Barker hissed. "You don't have a ticket, and you don't have an ID badge!"

Cody took a step into the room, keeping his foot against the bottom edge of the door. "I'm working for Chad Metcalf," he said in a hoarse whisper. "I don't need a ticket." Had Metcalf said nothing to her?

"I work for him too, and long before you did! Get the hell out! Everybody needs a ticket or a badge! That's the rule." When he didn't back up, she suddenly struck him in the abdomen with the heels of both hands. Other than the surprised look that came over Cody's face, this had no effect what-

ever, so she did it again. At the front, the presenter fell silent with an irritated look at a plot twist he
hadn't anticipated. People turned around. Cody
gripped Lola Barker's shoulder with one large hand
and turned her face and body against the wall,
where he held her in place with the other hand
pressing against the back of her neck. By this point
he had the full attention of everyone in the room.

"He's that detective cop," someone said. "I
was in his meeting this morning."

"I'm sorry to interrupt, and I won't take more
than a moment of your time." Lola Barker squirmed
under the pressure of his hand, breathing hard. Her
cheek was flattened against the plaster. Cody tried to
make it look quite natural that he'd be restraining
her in this way, as if she were an animal whose leash
had been broken or misplaced. "I have an important
message for Lisa Givens. Is she here this afternoon?"

People gaped at one another, shaking their
heads. After waiting a moment more, Cody realized he had caused this interruption for nothing, but
he and Paul hadn't been able to think of any other
way to find Lisa if she wasn't responding to phone
calls. He waited another thirty seconds for her to
stand up, but she didn't. Lola was straining to push
herself away from the wall with all her strength, and

he abruptly released his grip. With a gasp of surprise, and a tremendous thrust from her flexed upper arms, Lola achieved liftoff only to instantly sit down hard on the floor with the splat of ample flesh against rough limestone stiles.

Cody gave an apologetic wave and left, shutting the door softly behind him.

"Damn!" he said to himself. He couldn't recall ever getting so much resistance from the people he was trying to help. It made him wonder whether Chad Metcalf even knew what his own interest was. Or had Lola Barker made herself into a much larger force in the conference organization than Metcalf was aware of? Cody wondered whether he had now stumbled across the power behind the throne.

CHAPTER NINE

As she'd suggested, Maya had stayed home, burned out on the conference management. As a Méxican, she'd been shocked at the rudeness of her treatment from the gringos at the top, and it made her back off with her hands in the air, palms outward. She didn't give much credence to the normally negative stereotypes about how Americans behave in México, but there were times, like now, when I'm sure she was tempted to generalize about the ugly American. It was a shame, because we rarely encountered them here. I met Cody in the lobby of the Rosewood and we separated downstairs. I took on the cluster of small session rooms farther down the hall from him. Two out of three were occupied.

One was a pitch session where aspiring writers could sit down with a real agent for up to ten minutes and attempt to interest him in a book in progress, or at least in the planning stage. If the agent bit, he'd ask to see a chunk of it. I assumed that these meetings only happened on a one-to-one basis, which meant a low population turnover in that room. This made my job easier. After all, how many ID badges could I read as people rushed out? Since they were hung at breast level, and most of the attendees were women, in searching for Lisa Givens' name I would quickly be perceived as a masher with a mammary fixation, and Lola Barker would soon have me in the side-by-side crosshairs of her double-barreled contempt. The conference probably had a detention area further below grade where people who broke the rules could be systematically interrogated with exotic devices and dealt with according to the seriousness of their offense.

The other breakout session on my stubby corridor was titled *Character-driven Characters*. This sounded interesting to me, although I couldn't have said why—maybe because it didn't sound like a formula. This was also where I expected to nail Lisa Givens if Cody hadn't found her. She had reason to avoid me, although she couldn't have realized how much I already knew about her.

It was nearly 3:45, and the sessions were about to end. I positioned myself at the intersection of the short hallway and the main corridor, where I could more easily see the names on the conference badges as both rooms emptied. The light was better there. I didn't know what Cody was up to in the next cluster of rooms, but I hadn't heard any big disturbance, so either he hadn't found Lisa Givens, or if he had, she wasn't putting up a fight. In any case, I couldn't leave my position to find out.

Both doors opened simultaneously. Immediately, a man and a woman emerged from the agent pitch session. Once in the hallway they quickly separated. Their body language jointly suggested they were relieved to stop knowing each other, and with each step they took, the distance between them widened until they left the hallway hugging opposite walls. I was reminded of a line from Sartre's *No Exit*: Hell is other people. Sometimes you don't connect.

At the same time, a clot developed that blocked the door of the character-driven session across the hallway. This served my interests well. Once the pitch session woman had passed me, and I established that she was not Lisa Givens, I moved closer and gave the other group my detailed attention.

"No man would ever do that." I didn't see who said this, but it sounded interesting.

"But I don't need *every* man to act that way,"

one woman was saying indignantly to another, "all I need is that one does. I'm not dealing in stereotypes, here, OK? I think that's what he was saying just now. Clichés don't drive a story: they make the reader yawn. I'm writing a *literary* mystery. It'll be one that matters when all the other trash is gone." Her wide gesture took in the half-full room behind her. "Think of Sherlock Holmes." Clearly she'd never be held back by low self-esteem.

At this point I wished I had made notes from the Barlow notebook on what Lisa Givens' project was, because it had drifted right out of my head. Barlow's denunciations sounded so much alike that they caused everyone's works in progress to merge if you hadn't read them in detail.

At the exit of the character-driven room, the cork popped, and the cliché discussion group was elbowed aside as about a dozen and a half chattering people pushed their way out, notebooks in hand. I had a hole card here. It was that if Lisa Givens had attended our disastrous morning session of the day before, she would recognize me, and her body language might give her away even before I could glimpse her nametag. At that time, we still hadn't had any reason to think she might be avoiding us.

The rest of the room's inhabitants bulged

into the hallway and I couldn't make out more than about a quarter of the nametags. None of them I read belonged to Lisa Givens. I was standing at the left side of the opening on the main corridor, and at the right rear of the emerging knot of people a woman made uneasy eye contact with me. Then her face took on a startled look. When she shrank back, I lost sight of her. I started to force my way through the group in her direction, but from the corner of my eye I caught a flicker of movement at the periphery, and heard footsteps running in the direction of the lobby. Who else but Lisa would run away from me?

I struggled to untangle myself from the crowd, which now surrounded me, but by the time I did and launched myself running after her, the woman had a long start, and she was not holding anything back. As people leaped out of her way, I could see the flop of a blond ponytail on her neck as she ran, the up and down jiggle of her backpack, and her olive pants over black and white athletic shoes. As she reached the turn into the lobby, where she could exit onto the floor of the amphitheater outside with its two stairways leading to the main level, she barely slowed.

As I approached the other room cluster, where Cody had been working, I hit maximum speed with my arms pumping. Dodging conference attendees as

I flashed across the intersection, I took an unexpected impact on the front of my right ankle and found myself airborne. Momentum will take you only so far without any aerodynamics behind it, and I was soon skating across the unpolished limestone floor on my chest, knees, and hips, using my elbows as brakes. I'd left my wind behind me at the point of impact, not readily available as I came to a halt along the wall. People around me stopped also, mostly to assess my injuries in hushed voices.

I rolled over on my side with a groan and propped myself up on one arm, avoiding the elbow. There, with her feet anchored like those of a stubby gladiator, both fists on her hips, was Lola Barker. I was somehow not surprised. On her face, determination fought with triumph to form the nastiest look I'd ever seen on a human.

"There will be no more *running* in this corridor! Do you understand that? We have *rules* here! You cannot operate a conference of this importance without *rules*!" Her rigid index finger began to lash the air.

I noticed a broad reddish blotch covering one of her cheeks, and her nose appeared slightly flattened to the right, but at that point I was struggling for air and in no condition to be greatly observant on detail, especially when the whole Lola Barker package was so unappealing. All I wanted to do was groan.

It was only when I had partially recovered my breath that I could even gasp in response, "You silly bitch!" She wouldn't have heard it because, like a drum majorette, Lola was already stomping away down the corridor in rhythm with the defeated sighs of her next victims.

"That certainly was very rude, young man," said a slim, older woman in black slacks and a blue cotton top, as she helped me to my feet. "I saw that short woman stick her foot out in your path. In my day people had better manners than that."

"Thank you. Normally San Miguel isn't like this. I hope you didn't get the wrong impression." Sometimes, even pounded like that, I just shift into the goodwill ambassador role like some kind of chamber of commerce shill.

"Not at all. Something like this must draw a different crowd, and not the best quality, by the way. I come down here every year because my daughter lives here. Yes! She's not scared." The woman leaned in closer, reaching up to put her hand on my shoulder. "I'm not really a writer, but I'm a big reader, and I only came to the conference to see them, you know, the real writers. I just love that Dr. Ruth. I hope she writes another one."

"You could've fooled me; you're probably able to write rings around most people here." I said this as I hobbled away down the corridor, realizing that both of my knees had taken hits too. I planned to talk to Maya about putting a medical expense provision on Chad's bill. I began to wonder whether Lola Barker was covering something up, other than her own psychological scars, now in need of critical care. I made a note to speak with Cody about that. Naturally, speaking with Lisa Givens was no more than a distant and vanishing fantasy at that point. I hoped she was still running hard, badly out of breath, and that the water bottle in her backpack was empty.

It's possible that once my knees and elbows healed I'd be able to find some sympathy for Lola Barker as a victim of whatever demons in her past had forced her so firmly over to the dark side. Another, even more pressing, question was what kind of void lurked within Chad Metcalf that could be made whole by Lola Barker's demented presence. It was a yin and yang combination that I found unnerving, but it wasn't our main problem. The easy disappearance of Lisa Givens, our last promising suspect, was. I already knew from experience that it was hard to move on from your earliest suspect list and I couldn't bring myself to let go of Lisa.

The psychology department of the Paul Zacher Agency is staffed by Cody, but I hadn't seen him at the Rosewood after my fall. What was inside Lola's mind, other than fire and brimstone, I put off for a later session. After I'd rubbed my skinned and blunted joints for a while, (the new access through the holes in my shirt and jeans made that easy) I headed gingerly toward the Hacienda Old México, where Lisa was staying. Ancha de San Antonio was clotted with creeping vehicles, with one lane closed for a long block as the street laborers ripped up the irregular slate-like pavers and put them back down again. Part of me wanted to believe they each ended up back in the same position with the same kind of mosaic logic when they were finished. But I realized this thought reflected no more than my longing for an orderly world, something that hadn't been much in evidence lately. Meanwhile my need to find Lisa Givens increasingly possessed the urgency of teenage lust, if not the same intent.

Unfortunately my glimpse of her face in the

exiting crowd had been only partial, mainly her eyes growing in size as she recognized me. While I have a remarkable visual memory, the sighting occupied less than a second, so I didn't think it was enough to recognize her if I saw her again. The hotel desk clerk regarded me with a mixture of sympathy and suspicion as I limped up to the reception counter. I knew he was expecting me to ask whether they had handicapped rooms.

"Which room does Lisa Givens have? She's expecting me, please."

He gave me a skeptical look. "You are too late, *señor*. She checked out fifteen minutes ago. Perhaps she gave up waiting for you?"

I already knew without being reminded that I wasn't moving that fast. Without responding beyond a thank you, I settled on a loveseat nearby in the lobby and contemplated with gusto the final moments of Lola Barker. If she hadn't intervened, I would've caught up with Lisa Givens and I'd be talking to her now. I'd be moving this case forward without feeling I ought to be using a walker to get around.

Even though it was only two kilometers away, I spent twenty-five pesos to take a cab home, where I found that Cody and Maya had already begun cocktail hour. My joints were getting worse instead of better and Cody helped me to lower myself into my seat on the loggia while Maya made me a margarita and fetched a basket of meds. I told my pathetic story and Cody told his, and they dovetailed nicely. Cody had held Lola against the wall, and then, in revenge, she had dropped me on the floor from a dead run.

We had collectively gained nothing but injuries from our Rosewood visit, but Maya had come up with a small item that she was holding for my arrival. She opened Barlow's notebook and slid it between us, pointing to a tiny notation at the bottom of Amy Wendt's opening page. Cody pulled out his reading glasses.

At the bottom left corner we saw the note, *CM5C* in tiny letters. We now knew that Barlow had excellent vision, at least close up. His thick glasses were only for distance.

"I wish they were all this simple," Cody said. "C, of course, is the Roman numeral for 100."

"Right," said Maya, "and M stands for 1,000. So we have 100, 1000, 5—in an Arabic numeral—and 100. But when the smaller numeral is before the bigger one, you subtract it. So CM means 900. What's easy about that? I still don't get what it means."

"What I think is that it's more like Chad Metcalf (CM) 5C, or 500. Barlow must have paid

Metcalf $500 for bringing Amy in. Are there more notations like this?"

Maya nodded. "I spent some time on this today. Almost all of them have it, although Ruth Bendickson's page is one of a few that doesn't. Apparently Barlow signed up some clients on his own, although not from referrals, I imagine. Most of the time he paid Metcalf to recruit for him."

"And Chad," I said, "used his position as conference director to develop a nice referral business from his attendees."

"Excuse me, but Metcalf isn't on trial here," Cody said. "We work for him."

"Piffle. We've worked for the perpetrator before," I said. "Not that Chad is a real suspect—this causes way too much disorder for his tastes. We saw that. But remember when Antonio Trujillo hired us in the Malcolm Brendel case?"

"He only hired us for $10,000 to get you to tell him everything you knew about it," said Maya. "You were more like a consultant, giving him regular status updates, even though you didn't realize his role at the time."

"Excuse me, too, but I was still the head of the agency then."

"And you immediately turned against our client," added Cody, rather primly, I thought.

Now I began to understand better why I was no longer the head of the firm. "Not for the first time, and it'll probably happen again. Money only buys my time, not my soul. Anyway, Trujillo was a killer, remember?"

"Aren't you getting kind of lofty, Paul?" Maya asked. I realized she'd found a new word for her English slang lexicon, and a fairly good use for it.

"I tend to react that way when I've been kicked around too much."

"It's also called taking refuge in principle when violence is not an option as a response," said Cody. "In this case because you can't kick the shit out of that woman. I believe that Maya, had she been there, would've done exactly that. Even though Lola outweighs her by forty pounds, and is seven inches shorter."

Maya put her hand on Cody's arm in affirmation. "Being densely packed doesn't always make her formidable. She's a smaller target," she said, "and wider."

I understood this well enough, but still, there are times when I wish the Zacher Agency psychology department would shut its bloody window at siesta time like everything else here and give the rest of us a much-needed break. Sometimes it felt like nothing better than second-guessing the former chief executive.

We were about to move on to other things less troublesome, like when were the bananas against the north wall of the garden going to be ready for harvest, and why did they always grow upside down, when Cody raised one finger.

"There's another small thing," he said, "I asked Sheila to focus her psychic powers on the name of Amy Wendt. It took her by surprise, and that's usually good. That's how I like to do it, because then it's more likely that something will just jump into her mind. She responded with two words, 'Best seller.'"

"If only," said Maya, shaking her head sadly. "That girl was taken down by her despair before she ever had a chance to make that happen. Anyway, bestseller is a single word. I already looked it up on the off chance I'd ever get to use it for my own book."

CHAPTER TEN

The following morning I knocked unannounced on Chad Metcalf's office cubicle door. I still had a lot of aches and pains, but I was moving better after taking four ibuprofen tablets before breakfast, on top of the four I'd taken before I went to bed. At least I'd slept well. In any case, I was too proud to use a cane. It was about 10:15. I figured the ten o'clock breakout sessions had started and he wouldn't be introducing anyone at the moment.

"Oh, it's you," he said graciously, and opened the door farther. I went in and sat down. "You must've made some progress, right?" I felt like my stock was in a dip.

"A little. The autopsy on Justus Barlow indicated he died from an overdose of his own heart medication, Digoxin."

Metcalf clapped his hands. "That's great! So,

it *was* an accident. That was my second choice, after his being so excited to be here that he had a heart attack—although my publicist had a great idea on that too. He suggested we could trumpet the angle that if it really was a murder at a mystery writers' conference, then we solved it in-house right away. The press would go absolutely nuts with it. I could tweet it and it would go viral. I've got people following me on Twitter that have 200,000 followers of their own—I make a point of that. So all I do is put it up, and bang, they retweet me into the cloud. I'm like Jesus ascending into heaven, but with a bigger audience and more impact. It's the echo that goes around the world. This new technology is so powerful! What do you think?"

I had no idea what he was talking about. "It *was* a murder, Chad, not an accident. Barlow had eight times the normal dose of that medication in his bloodstream. He would've had to swallow a small handful of pills to get that much, and he knew the risks. I saw the date on his prescription bottle, and it was first issued more than four years ago. He must have renewed it a dozen times. If he was going to screw up like that, he would've done it long ago."

"I'll be damned! But you don't think it could've been suicide?" Metcalf probed the cleft in his chin with a fingernail and inspected the result.

"So he kills himself as he was standing on the podium during an anti-adverb rant? I don't think so. I saw the first part of it, and he was triumphant. He was in the zone up there."

"Well, now that we know where we stand, your job is to solve it before the police do. Then we can still claim that the conference was way ahead of law enforcement on this—that's how good we are! We can teach the police their jobs, for Christ's sake! Especially down here with these local rubes like Delgado. I'll tell my PR guy to draft the press releases so they can go out as soon as you wrap it up. Then I'll get the tweets ready. I love the way this is going, don't you?" He took a moment to rub his hands together. They gave off the pinkish aura of scented lotion. I wondered whether they had ever gotten dirty.

"No, I don't, Chad. I don't care for it at all. We're getting a little information mixed with a lot of obstruction from Lola Barker. Yesterday she tripped me when I was in a dead run after a suspect in this case. Because of her interference, we lost an important opportunity, to say nothing about what my knees and elbows look like now. I need you to tell me whose side that woman is on, because the way it's going, if the murderer came up and pulled a gun on us, my guess is that she'd be standing next to him handing him more ammunition."

"Oh, that." He waved the issue away as if I was inflating the problem. When he saw that my sour expression hadn't changed, he leaned forward across the desk with a secret. "I want you to know that Lola Barker takes her job very seriously, some might even say too seriously."

My expression didn't change. "Tell me this. Is she related to Ma Barker, like maybe a daughter? She has definitely got the same kind of genes."

"Cute. But what you're *not* seeing here, Paul, and I understand why, is that I run this show with a batch of damn greenhorn volunteers that I have to assemble every year from scratch in each new location. Imagine that! Do you think that's any fun for me? That is what my job will be starting next week, when I get back to New York. Unlike on the golf tournaments I run, where I can charge higher entrance fees, I use very few paid professionals. This time next year, we'll be in Maui, doing a rerun of this program. Of course, we'll have a different lead speaker. Confidentially," here his voice dropped to a whisper, "I'm thinking either Bob Crais or Tony Hillerman."

"Tony Hillerman is dead, Chad." I knew this

only because Maya had told me. She had liked the way he used Native Americans as lead characters in his mysteries.

Chad waved this off. "Whatever, so the man missed his chance with us. I don't care—I'm used to rejection. But trust me, Crais'll leap at it, I've met his agent."

"I've heard that Robert Crais uses a lot of adverbs. Are you sure you want him?" Of course, I knew nothing of the sort. Maya had read Crais and liked him, but I never had.

"Bob Crais does, Paul. Yes, he does—and you nailed him on that. Good eye, by the way." Chad Metcalf's voice again dropped to a confidential whisper. "But the difference is that he uses them all *well*. I've read everything of his. And what my friend Justus Barlow never got a chance to say, but I know damned well he was building up to it when he was so rudely cut down, was that a way back exists for the adverb. That was the surprise ending to his speech. In fact, this could be the theme of next year's conference—the return of the adverb, in Maui. Great idea, eh? How do I know this? Because Justus Barlow, the man, if he stood for any single thing at all, was all about hope. Hope and change." The filmy moisture in Metcalf's eyes threatened to escape at this point. "Redemption was absolutely his mantra! He was a dear soul, and I was so privileged to know him as I did during the brief time he was with us. You would've liked him, by the way. Deep down, you and Justus are the same kind of person, cut from the same cloth—and I know I'm flattering you there, because, for both of you, it's all about integrity. Don't ask me how I know this, I just do." So many gestures accompanied this statement that I thought that several of his rings were about to fly off his fingers.

I studied Chad Metcalf for a long moment, as many others must have done before me, locking in a neutral expression. Even as long as I've been in México, understanding what I'm looking at can still sometimes be a challenge, but when it is, it usually involves things Méxican. Rarely do I look at an American without any comprehension at all of what I'm seeing, but Metcalf truly had me stumped. I probably should have sent Cody to do this conversation in his role as chief of the agency psychology division. Or maybe I should go back to the States more often to check what was going on there. Had something essential changed over the border? I had no idea. When I moved away, Bill Clinton was planning his second term. Hilary had been pounded for her attempt to remake health care. We all know how the second Clinton term came out: the Republicans soiled themselves trying to remove him from office. I hadn't paid much attention since then, with good reason. When Maya wanted to watch the Academy Awards, mainly to see the dresses, I usually couldn't make it through to the end because I didn't recognize most of the people on stage, and I couldn't remember their names after they were introduced. I'd never seen any of the movies.

"There's one thing, above all others, that I would like you to take away from this conversation, Paul. And by the way, it's a damned important one."

"Only one?"

"Several, really, but one especially. Lola Barker is a key part of my team." As if we were getting down to basics, he pointed with a single finger at the desk surface before him, as if on that plastic laminate was where the fundamentals were to be found. "She's been with me quite a while. You have suggested that her presentation is neither the most welcoming nor the most polished you've ever seen, but she was never the teddy bear type, I'll give you that. The woman has her issues. If she were a Biblical character, for example, she'd be wearing a hair shirt, and enjoying it. Maybe she is anyway, I wouldn't know. But have you ever considered that such a façade—that's how I think of it—is intentional, a calculated effect? That it's been planned that way, even for a long time?"

"Yes I have, Chad. In fact, that's why I'm here, asking these awkward questions. But listen to this—no matter how much time you spend admiring yourself in the mellow sheen of her jackboots, Lola still works against your interests in solving this case, and against the interests of your conference. Most important now, she also works against the interests of the Paul Zacher Agency, which you have hired to get your ass out of this muddy hole. She's costing you a lot of money every day—it's your meter that's ticking, not mine."

Chad Metcalf leaned back in his chair, and stuck a finger deeply into one of his cheek dimples. The nail disappeared inside. Chuckling, he gave me a benign smile and then folded his hands over his chest. It was as if a knot of very young children was rushing with no result whatever against the base of his ivory throne.

CHAPTER ELEVEN
MAYA SANCHEZ

L ater that day, Maya was driving the Dolores Hidalgo road on her way to a two o'clock luncheon appointment with Ruth Bendickson. Earlier at the Rosewood Hotel, the writer had participated in an 11:30 panel discussion on the subject of *The Future of the Mystery Novel*. Accompanying her on the platform were a New York editor from a failing publishing house in search of a merger, and two other mystery writers of lesser popularity, whose total combined sales were a tenth of what Ruth's were on any single book. Now lacking a credential, Maya had attended by slipping into the ballroom unseen from the staff entrance, where Méxicans were invisible. Keeping a low profile, she hadn't asked any questions or tried to speak with Ruth afterwards. She knew her moment was coming later.

Paul had returned from his meeting with

Chad Metcalf ready to chew rusty nails, and Cody had gone down to the *jardín* (the plaza, in local terms) police office to see Diego Delgado about trying to get some help finding Lisa Givens.

On the previous day there had been a discussion within the agency about which of them might be best suited for the Ruth Bendickson interview. Cody felt his long experience would qualify him the most, since a person in Ruth's position could be somewhat formidable. He would at least be the same height, and part of Ruth's strength was that she dominated everyone around her. Maya felt she was a better fit because she'd read Ruth's three mysteries and the others hadn't, nor had they ever read any mysteries at all. Cody felt he'd lived one most of his professional life, and Paul, pursuing his own visual mysteries, didn't care. Maya also argued that she spoke the language, knew the jargon and the medium. Moreover, as a woman, her presence would be less confrontational. Paul supported this idea. Cody yielded, as he always did to her.

Maya also had an undisclosed agenda in meeting with the popular author. In the process of reading mysteries over the past two or three years, she had developed a clear set of ideas about what she thought worked and what didn't. Also at the back of her mind were the nine prior cases of the Zacher Agency and their potential value as raw material. She knew that her own biography on the early days of Ignacio Allende gave her writing skills credibility. Elaborating and fictionalizing recent events, instead of drawing them from the historical research materials, was something she'd often felt like doing, but never had because writing history has a different set of rules. There were times when she thought Paul might have figured this out, but she wasn't ready to go public with it yet. Sitting down face to face with Ruth Bendickson would give her, she hoped, a better sense of that process, away from the crowds of the older writer's admirers. At the panel discussion the audience members had been allowed only a single question each, and Ruth's answers had consistently been brief.

About eight kilometers out of San Miguel, Maya turned left at the exit for el Cortijo, where the hot springs in this area begin. El Cortijo is a small village fronted by walled properties on both sides of the road. One is a convent where local people at risk of starvation can ring a bell, and a nun will bring them a meal, packaged "to go." The most prominent feature is the Parador el Cortijo, a rambling, white stucco hotel that looks like 1940. Gringos who search for

such things take it to be the real México, where the
women wear flowers in their hair and the men sport
big sombreros over mariachi costumes. The reality is
that it caters mostly to big city Méxicans in designer
jeans and Ralph Lauren shirts who come to take the
thermal baths. They often drive Audis or BMWs.
These formations meander through central México
up toward the city of Lagos de Moreno, and beyond, into Aguas Calientes, which means hot waters.

Passing over the speed bump near the
parador gate, Maya had a sudden startling insight.
In her musings about mining the agency files for
raw material, she had always focused on the clients
and the perpetrators. Rarely had she pictured Paul
or Cody in the frame, and certainly never herself.
In her mind, she suddenly drew back with a quea-
sy feeling. While this was an obvious oversight that
would've instantly come to light had she discussed
it with Paul, just recognizing it now spotlighted her
own sense of privacy. Although she enjoyed her appearance in the mirror, and had never minded posing
nude for Paul, she recoiled from the idea portraying
herself on the page. Would the narrative be in the first
person or the third, I or she? Maya had been active in too many cases to conceal her role. And what
would she say about Paul or about Cody? How far

could she go with their private truth? There had been cases that were extremely personal and painful. The episode with Yasmin Montoya, who was actually the subject of a missing person search at the time, was the most difficult of all because Paul had gotten involved with her romantically after Maya left him for three months. Some situations had been papered over without ever being fully worked out. Méxican families, and she considered her relationship with Paul to be one, had a consistency like bread rising, full of explosive bubbles and turbulent yeasty fulminations that you wouldn't want to have publicly breaking through to the surface. She began to wonder how Ruth Bendickson handled questions like this. Had she appeared in her own books, even in heavy disguise? Was it as thick as stage makeup? Did you act differently if you didn't quite look like yourself? If Maya hadn't been on the way to an appointment, she would've pulled off the road to work this through further without the distraction of driving.

About half a kilometer in, the el Cortijo road forks, leading on the right toward the pre-Cortés village of Atotonilco, with its legendary pilgrimage shrine, and on the left onto a rough washboard route that doubles back in the direction of San Miguel.

Along this unpaved track, which launched

volumes of dust behind her, Maya passed the remains of an ancient hacienda with its humpbacked roofline, suggesting a series of rooms inside with *bóveda* ceilings. Across the road a cluster of stone worker's houses from the eighteenth century had once been attached to the estate. Finally, a number of more important properties came into view. The last in this series was a manicured agricultural domain of many hectares with a large, thatched-roof residence that would have looked more at home in the Yucatan. Still preoccupied, Maya drove through the gate and along groomed fields of organic crops into the parking area, where she pulled in next to a freshly buffed Mercedes 320 SUV.

It was a brilliant, cloudless day, full of promise, but she needed to focus on Ruth Bendickson again, rather than her own ambitions in detective fiction. Maya didn't know what to expect, yet she felt relatively comfortable. I'm not nervous, she announced to herself. She was wearing her best jeans with sequins and seed pearls on the back pockets, and a bottle-green blazer over a sleeveless white cotton knit top. As she got out of the van, a young man in a starched jacket emerged from the house and greeted her before leading her around to the other side, where a table was set for lunch on a shady terrace.

Twenty meters beyond, the ground fell sharply away into the valley of the Rio Laja, providing, on the river's lazy curve, a wide-angle view into the hills on the other side, dotted with prickly pear cactus and agave. The nearer edge was defined by a low wall topped by succulents in large clay pots.

With a casual wave, Dr. Ruth emerged from the house, where four pairs of French doors opened toward the valley. Wearing a pale tan linen pants suit, she extended her hand to Maya.

"Thank you for seeing me today," Maya said. "What a lovely spot!"

"Not a problem. Chad asked me to meet with you. Normally I don't see people individually. Do you know this house?"

"It belongs to the Wilsons, doesn't it? I think they're active in several service groups in town."

Dr. Ruth shrugged vaguely. "They're very nice, and he's a big person in fashion in Miami too, I think. Fashion has never treated me that well; I think my wardrobe requires too much fabric, and it's all gotten so much more minimal in recent years. Chad knows them somehow in that way he has of knowing everyone who matters. They went up to New York on Tuesday, but they were gracious enough to let me stay here for a few more days. It's fully staffed, of course.

Please sit down, won't you?" She gestured to the table.

Ruth Bendickson had a high-pitched nasal voice that Maya had already found disconcerting at the cocktail reception, and again at the panel discussion. Its nanny-like wheeziness was too frivolous for the writer's size. She wore two silver rings on each hand, but no other jewelry. Her ginger hair was short and layered. Maya thought it looked thin but carefully tended. Ruth's pale hazel eyes bounced from point to point, never lingering long. The impression she gave at any moment was that she might have been slightly bored.

"Would you like a glass of wine before we begin?" she asked. "I usually have one about this time. I always do my work in the morning, and now I'm off duty."

As if on cue, the houseboy appeared and took their order for two glasses of chardonnay.

Beyond the presence afforded by Dr. Ruth's sheer size, which Maya found hard to get used to, she wasn't getting much from her yet, but it was early in the conversation. "I've read all your books," Maya said, seeking to direct it. "*Rachel's Folly* is my favorite."

"Thank you for that so much! I think it was the most fun to write, and that's always apparent to

199

the reader. I knew early on it had to be a trilogy. Have you been attending the conference?"

Maya was surprised to be directed away from the subject of the book so quickly. She expected Ruth Bendickson would want to go on and on about it. Maya herself felt ready to speak at length whenever the subject of her own Ignacio Allende biography came up. Maybe the older writer was by now burned out on her earlier work, after endless signings and bookstore appearances. Besides, her current project must now be at least three books further on.

"Yes, I saw the panel discussion this morning." Maya didn't want to get into the Zacher Agency's humiliating ejection from the conference.

The houseboy set down a plate of rice crackers with tiny squares of seaweed on the top of each, and two glasses of wine in front of them.

"But I understand from Chad that you came here to talk about Justus Barlow. What an unfortunate man! He certainly had developed his own niche, but he was deeply flawed, nonetheless." She sighed and stared across the river valley. "Of course people like that make the most interesting characters."

"How did you come to know him?" Maya didn't introduce this by asking whether she Ruth knew him, hoping to get a more spontaneous reaction, but Dr. Ruth's response was seamless.

"Some time back—it must have been about six years ago now—Justus gave a talk at Bolton College, in Connecticut, where I was teaching. I'm still on the faculty there. I remember it so well. His subject was self-editing, a rare skill indeed. Most new writers are too self-indulgent to attempt it, or, frankly, even to see the need for it. It's as if each sentence has been dictated to them by God, and then carved in stone. I'm not certain how much my students in the audience learned from it, because it went so much against their inclinations." Here Ruth leaned back in her chair and smiled. "That evening, however, several of us from the English Department faculty had dinner with Justus at an intimate bistro in Greenwich. I can recall that we all looked forward to it. I think each of us at that table was a writer, or a would-be writer. I didn't organize it, but that was how it came together."

"What impressed you most about him?"

"That's easy. I thought he was hard headed, with a nuts and bolts kind of approach I appreciated. Let me say here that I've never been a fan of mystique in writing or in anything else. I had a fiction project going myself that had been bogged down for years and, halfway through the dinner, I began to wonder whether Justus couldn't help me move it forward. I had actually never thought seriously about getting help with it before."

Ruth Bendickson had a way of ending her sentences on an up-sloping ramp, as if they were questions. She took a long pull at the chardonnay and after she set it down, put one hand over the other on the table, looking frankly at her guest. It signaled a new level of intimacy for the conversation.

"The truth is that I was blocked, Maya. I was stopped cold, and I was very upset about it. Yet being upset hadn't helped me get back into it. If anything, the effect was the opposite. Every time I sat down to work I had a visceral reaction and I'd freeze up. Of course, now, after the Rachel trilogy is in print, it's so much easier to talk about. But at that time, you won't be surprised if I say I expected more from myself. Because I was senior faculty at Bolton, and advising dozens of young writers about the process of writing, many of them MFA candidates, I hadn't felt able to talk frankly to anyone there about it. Justus Barlow, as an outsider, and a New York editing professional, suddenly looked like someone I could work with, but still not lose face while I was doing it, do you see? Subject, of course, to his being discreet."

Maya nodded and gave her a reassuring

smile. She realized that Ruth would never be speaking this frankly if her books hadn't been so successful—it went beyond simply being in print. "And was he discreet?"

"Always. A lack of discretion was never his failing. It came easily because he was a recluse, and I don't think he ever saw many people he wasn't working with."

"We have his client notebook. It says your manuscript was called, *These Things Are Mine.*"

She gave a high-pitched laugh, rather like a colt neighing. "Oh, right. It sounds a little emphatic now, doesn't it? I had titled it early on, in a more optimistic frame of mind, but by the time I was working with Justus, my feelings about it were far more tentative." She smiled grimly. "As I quickly came to understand from working with him, it should've properly been titled, *These Things Are Going Nowhere.*"

Maya chuckled politely. "Did he like it at all? I've heard he could be tough on his clients. I'm not sure whether you realized they were all women."

Ruth Bendickson shrugged and took a small sip of her wine, as if she was now pacing herself better for a conversation that might go into the subject with more depth than she was accustomed to, or would normally have allowed. At a subtle signal from her left hand, the server came back to the table. "Bring the salad now, Javier, and water with ice. And a bowl of those Greek olives, I think? You never put enough in for my taste." She waited until he was gone before she spoke again. "You're right about him selecting only women. I knew Justus was too harsh with some of them for no better reason than that he could get away with it, but he never was with me. Without my saying so, I think he understood from the beginning that I would've decked him." She said this with no emphasis, as if it were something anyone who was planning to do business with her ought to realize in advance.

Startled, Maya paused for a moment before she could continue. She wondered whether being a woman of this size brought with it a degree of physicality other women couldn't aspire to.

"Did you already know Chad Metcalf then?"

"I'm sure I must have. Everybody knows Chad."

"Did you meet him through Justus Barlow?"

"I may have. I don't recall now. Chad's a fixture in this business. Working these conferences is an established promotional venue for a lot of writers, so it would be difficult to avoid him if you were marketing a book."

"Is that how you look at it? As a business?"

Ruth gave Maya a smile that suggested her long experience in writing and publishing had brought a seasoned realism with it. "Of course, both the writing part and the running of conferences. Whatever else could it be? Once you're inside it, you'd never romanticize it. Calling it a den of thieves would be too polite."

Taken aback, and thinking of her own labor of passion on her Allende book, Maya was unable to respond to this directly. "But Chad's not a writer himself, is he?"

"No, no, never. Few at this conference are. Haven't you noticed that?" She gave Maya the look of an insider, not quite ironic, but not naïve and open either. "At the Rosewood we have an innocent terrain inhabited by wannabes, like newborn rabbits in a meadow on a May morning. All the sharp objects of reality have been removed before their arrival. Do you rub shoulders with writers in those corridors? Never! The wannabes rub shoulders with you. They're mainly there to feel good about themselves, not because they've written anything recently, or ever. But in coming to the conference they will *see* real writers in the flesh, they will observe them at close quarters. They'll know how writers walk, how they eat their dinner, how they speak, and when they leave, going back to Tulsa or Billings or Montgomery, they'll have the feeling that they are now part of a community. They are one in spirit with real writers only because they have briefly inhabited the same space with them, the same building, but not in any other way. Of course, none of this is about writing. The few real writers are there to promote their books, just as I am. The rest merely fantasize. Conferences like this fuel dreams, rather like Las Vegas in the wee hours."

Almost stunned, Maya regarded her for a moment in silence. Ruth had spoken as if this had been an old conclusion of hers, but Maya saw it as a genuine insight. Writing had been a welcome and rewarding task on her own first book, and in her mind she was now broadening out the future possibilities, but she'd never thought of herself in this way, even falsely, as a member of a supportive community. She knew no other writers, and none had ever offered her their help or encouragement. Two or three times she'd been startled to think that people envied her achievement. Her efforts had always been solitary, and unique in her experience. Determined to reexamine it later, she put the thought aside and returned to the interview.

"What led you to abandon *These Things Are Mine?*"

Ruth made an offhand gesture, as if brushing aside a troublesome fly near her cheek. "After a few initial conversations, in which I was feeling increasingly despondent about that book, Justus convinced me it wasn't worth saving. When I told him I'd started it thirteen years earlier and still only had a quarter of it in first draft, he advised me to begin a different project. I was approaching fifty at that point, Maya, and the idea of making a fresh start on what still would only have been my first book seemed daunting."

As if visualizing that time, she paused and looked over the valley of the Rio Laja. The river itself was not visible from where they sat, but the empty space above it gave the feeling of a broad perspective, a viewpoint cleared of any obstacle. "On the other hand, the thought of going back and taking another run at my stalled manuscript was even worse. He made me face the fact that I was by that time sick to death of it, that the book had become a load of baggage that was weighing me down. He showed me that I'd be able to bring more vigor and energy to a fresh concept. Not that I knew what it might be at that point."

There was nothing in what Maya had seen in the notebook to contradict this. "And that was valuable." She knew it was, but she wanted to nudge the conversation along in the same direction, after feeling she'd been deflected earlier about the first Rachel book.

"Extremely. Justus made me see that if you've practically memorized what you've done by going over it again and again so many times, looking for something, *anything*, to improve, it's never going any farther. You've already said everything you have to say, even if the story hasn't been told. Of course, none of that was obvious until I stopped resisting it. It took me a while to come to terms with his advice and change course. There was a painful process of letting go of the dream I'd had for that book. I'm sure you can see that. Every writer works from a dream, don't you think?"

For an instant Maya thought Ruth had looked into her mind. "And did he then help you with *Rachel's Folly*, once you'd started on it?" Barlow's notebook hadn't mentioned anything about that book, but it didn't always refer to a manuscript by its final title, which could always change as the project developed.

Dr. Ruth gave her a knowing smile and shook

her head. When she spoke, her voice held the sense of a sea change, of a tipping point passed. Her head tilted to one side. "No. I had the very good sense not to use Justus Barlow again. Our sessions on that first book had told me what I needed to know, and in *Rachel's Folly*, I didn't repeat my earlier mistakes. Even better, working with him had gotten me jump-started, once I'd mentally written off *These Things Are Mine*. As he'd suggested, I discovered I had far more energy, and I felt I didn't need him after that. When I heard from Chad that Justus was going to be here at this conference, I was excited to see him because I hadn't spoken to him in nearly six years. Frankly Maya, I was ready to dangle my triumph in front of his nose. He was often so insulated, I wasn't even sure he'd ever heard about it."

"So you did see him?"

"Actually not. I meant to connect with him when the presentations began, but then he died that first morning and I never had a chance. I'm sorry for him, but it would have been so sweet to sit there and talk about how much progress I'd made as a writer. Of course, he probably would've claimed credit for it. That was always his way, but even so."

Maya left a small space in the conversation, but Ruth didn't appear to need to compose herself any further about his loss. Of course, it had been a long time since she'd seen him.

"You haven't worked these conferences before."

"Others, but not this one. Chad would be the first to tell you that a fresh face is required for the keynote speaker each time. It's got to be different at the top for the participants, but Justus and several others at a lower level have been regulars with him since it started, or so Chad told me. Recently he's added some sessions about self-publishing. You know, he used to look down on that so much. It never seemed legitimate to him. He always tries to be so classy."

Maya wanted to probe this further, but she didn't, thinking it was not fully germane. "Going back to six years ago, or even after, were you aware of anyone who might have wanted to kill him?"

Ruth Bendickson leaned forward over her salad and set down her fork. "Are you really convinced he was murdered? I know that's your business, but if I remember correctly, Justus had a heart condition of some kind, and even back when I was working with him, he kept his medication nearby. The overall impression I had from him was never one of vigor or good health. I would have said then if you'd asked me, that he ran on mental energy. He had been injured somehow as a child, I never knew the detail of it, but he grew up feeling not quite equal to his peers. Naturally he was bullied. I got this indirectly from things he said now and then."

"We're not certain yet that it was murder, but at this point, that's our focus. The autopsy report says that he overdosed on his medication. I think that's difficult to do if you've been used to taking it for some time. Most people would quickly learn what the risks are. Besides, a number of his clients apparently had an experience with him less beneficial than yours. If it was murder, we're trying to understand whether one of his clients might have killed him over the character of his input. He was known for his abrasive approach. Would that be correct in your view?"

"I did hear that some others had a rougher time than I did, but I'm not aware of anyone who would've wanted to kill him. And as I said, I haven't seen him in years, so who knows what hidden reserves of animosity he might have built up in the meantime among his clientele? I think that in general—and as a writer, you won't be surprised at this—abusive people tend to get *more* abusive, not less, over time. That's certainly the way I'd write him if he were a character in one of my books. The reader would have felt he was heading toward his comeuppance, as he apparently was in life. If you're right about it being murder, someone out there is celebrating today."

They finished their salad of baby greens in silence. Maya rose and pulled off her blazer as the afternoon grew warmer. "There was another odd thing," she said, draping it over the back of her chair. Javier the houseboy rushed out with a padded hanger and took it away. "Someone gave us an anonymous tip that we should look into another client of Barlow's named Amy Wendt. Did you ever know her? It was a few years back, and roughly about the time you were using him."

After a flash of initial surprise, Ruth took a moment to compose her face. Maya was not able to interpret her look as Ruth shook her head.

"I wondered if you knew about Amy, but of course, she would have appeared in Justus's notebook with the rest of us. That poor girl was a tragedy waiting to happen. I met her at his office twice. I talked to her then, coming and going, and I felt she was a bad match for him as a client, but I never dreamed she'd kill herself. Teaching creative writing as I do, I'd met her type a number of times before. I thought of her as both troubled and talented. But that's not a rare combination with writers."

"What was she like?"

"I recall her well. She was an intense, mousy girl in her mid twenties or so. Not attractive, with a shadow on her upper lip and a messy ponytail with parts of it escaping. I felt her hair never looked all that clean. She had round cheeks and brown eyes under bushy eyebrows that could've used some grooming. Overall, she possessed what impressed me as a startled look. Maybe her eyes were too big, or they stuck out too much. The detail is getting away from me now, although I nearly used her as a character once. I always felt she didn't care much how she looked."

"When did you find out she had killed herself?" As a more emotional Méxican, Maya knew that in speaking with gringos she needed to maintain a neutral tone similar to theirs. It often required restraint.

"I didn't hear about it until after I was finished with Justus. I think someone on the faculty at Bolton might have told me." Dr. Ruth's tone was as neutral as Maya's.

"Do you think Barlow could have been indirectly responsible for her death?"

Ruth shook her head. When she replied, her diction was precise. "I think that Amy Wendt herself was responsible for that. I don't believe anyone can make you kill yourself. Justus might have been the catalyst if Amy was already at that point, I don't know. There have been plenty of suicides among other writers who had much more going on than Amy did. Think of Virginia Woolf, Ernest Hemingway, Sylvia Plath. The list must be immense. Did they all have their very good reasons? One assumes so, but we'll never know from the notes they left behind, which tend to be sparse."

"Did Barlow know that Amy had killed herself?"

"We didn't ever talk about it, since, as I said, at that point I was already gone from his life. Because his social skills were virtually nonexistent, he wasn't a person you stayed in contact with as a friend. Well, Chad did, but Chad has a knack for attracting some rather strange people. I assumed that Justus did know about Amy, if one day she simply didn't come back, but then you never knew what he was aware of and what he wasn't. He could tune things out easily. His organizational skills were extremely modest. Since you have his notebook, you already know that. Beyond email, I don't think he even knew much about operating a computer."

Maya thought of the word *DEAD* in Barlow's notebook. "In spite of that, do you think he had the ability to take a broad view of things?"

Ruth smiled ironically. "That would have been rare indeed. He was always standing in a hole. Even looking out over the edge would've been a challenge for Justus Barlow."

Not a problem you'd ever have, thought Maya, but was the perspective better from that height? Probably.

The houseboy brought a second glass of wine for each of them.

"Don't misunderstand me, though, Maya. I do give Justus some credit. He jump-started my writing career at a time when it was nearly dead, although I didn't realize it. Perhaps in my case, it was only a small insight on his part that made him able to do that; I don't know. It might even have been no more than luck, but I tend to measure people's actions by their effects more than by their intent. I wouldn't be sitting here today without Justus Barlow's input at that critical moment."

"In American terms, then, on a scale of one to ten, what was that input worth to you?"

Ruth did not hesitate. "Easily a six or seven in its effect, because the real effort that followed and made *Rachel's Folly* happen was still all mine. The important thing was this: you could never write him off. He might be foul, he might sneer at you and try to score points at your expense, he might make sexual advances if you were young and pretty—yes, I did hear that, too—but if you wrote him off entirely, it would be at your own cost. As with many others in this business, his output required a lot of editing, but there were always worthwhile nuggets in it. Amy Wendt was apparently unable to distinguish between the parts that were worthless and those she could put to good use. Maybe her skin just wasn't thick enough to be his client." Ruth's eyebrows went up in special emphasis.

Maya underlined this final phrase in her mind, thinking it might play some key role later with another suspect. "What are you working on now?"

A subtle cloud passed over Ruth's features and she spent a moment or two trying to find the right words. "I have a new character, and I'm still trying to flesh her out before I get too deeply into the narrative. She's fighting me, but she has great potential. After three books, four really, I've learned that if a project doesn't talk back to you at times, it may not be worth listening to. The struggle is a sign that it has a life of its own."

"Are you confident of winning that fight?"

An ironic smile formed on her lips. "Ah, that's at the core of it, always. Some critics will tell you I didn't win it with my third book. I don't know whether that's correct or not. When I wrapped it up I truly felt that I had." Ruth Bendickson gave a long sigh and finished her wine in a long draught. "Posterity will be the judge, I suppose. But I do know that there was a time in my life when I was *great*, and it was not so very long ago." She spoke slowly. "Maybe I'm not great anymore, and my grandest days are in the past, but in those first two books, I surely had that moment. And don't think I didn't know then that it was the sweetest part of my life."

Maya was still toying with her wine. She digested this for a moment, trying to recall whether she needed to ask anything more when she already had so much to digest. Returning to the present, Ruth watched her expectantly and with no embarrassment at her last statement. "Will there be anything else?"

"Just one more thing, a detail. Does the conference provide insurance for the principal presenters? I'm thinking of you, especially."

Ruth evidently regarded this as a joke. "Performance insurance? Not our boy Chad. He's too cheap. If there ever were to be a problem, he'd probably send someone to break your kneecaps. You might have to give your talk from a wheelchair, but you would indeed show up. Of course, Lola Barker would be watching so Chad could keep his hands clean. He likes to have deniability, and she's his dark side."

A moment later Dr. Ruth signaled Javier to show Maya to her car, and they said goodbye. He rushed out with her jacket on his arm. As Maya was about to round the corner of the house, she looked back and saw Ruth still seated at the garden table, staring off over the valley. She poured herself the final glass of wine from the bottle that Javier had left in a sterling ice bucket on the table.

Driving out through the irrigated fields of green, Maya was surprised at how much of Ruth Bendickson's mind she'd been allowed to see. The writer obviously had an official persona that may have been all she'd planned to show, but at the same time Maya felt she'd revealed a number of insights into her own Barlow experience as well as her career after she'd parted from him. Official or not, she hadn't come across as veiled at the end.

But had the conversation served its purpose? It had probed the literary aspects of Ruth's life more than Maya expected or Ruth herself intended. Yet, when two writers were talking about writing, how could that fail to happen?

In other ways, it was not so useful. It would

have been interesting to know what Barlow had done after Amy Wendt's suicide. There might have been some follow up with her family. Cody's information from Michael Wendt appeared to suggest there had been no contact after Amy's death.

Maya was left with the sense that, although Ruth Bendickson had achieved her great success later in life, she'd had no trouble coming to terms with it. It sounded like she had easily digested her Barlow experience, unlike some of his other clients, and quickly moved on. Even if she hadn't known exactly what she was looking for when she signed on with him, she'd easily recognized it when it appeared.

CHAPTER TWELVE

Cody came for dinner that night. We nearly always had our progress meetings at our house on Quebrada, because Cody's only private outdoor space was the shallow third-floor balcony of his condo, which could accommodate no more than three chairs, and those only in a row facing outward. It worked fine for bird watching. I grilled chicken fajitas and we briefed each other during dinner on the loggia. The sun had gone below our garden wall, although the light hadn't yet failed. It had developed a more orange cast where it lit the upper parts of the bamboo. Somewhere down the block a neighbor's chickens were settling in for the night with the usual bickering, and a roof dog challenged passersby on the street with his best big dog voice. I knew the dog in question and he had never weighed as much as fifteen kilos. Further down, someone hooted with glee at finding a parking place. It was evening in San Miguel.

"One of the things that struck me when I was talking to her," Maya said, "was that Ruth walked away from Barlow just like Dina Bauer did. She lost her first book in the process, but I think she was glad of that, since it was never going to work. She's a realist, and she dealt with it up front. She mentioned it was a struggle to give it up, but once she was reconciled to it, she was rolling again."

Cody dashed some *pico de gallo* onto his fajita. "You're suggesting our killer was someone who couldn't walk away. It's like a quick draw contest among the old West gunfighters. If you don't walk away, someone dies. So, what separates those who could walk away without drawing their six shooter from those who couldn't?"

"Knowing who you are," I said. "Being secure in your identity. You don't need to prove anything by trying to gun down someone else, or be gunned down in the process. Another notch on your pistol grip isn't meaningful anymore, even if it once was."

"Ruth would probably say that it's the thickness of their skin," said Maya. "She speculated that Amy Wendt's skin was too thin to take the criticism, but she still couldn't walk away from Barlow."

"But killing herself was certainly different

than killing Barlow," I offered.

"I don't think it was that much different," said Cody. "In either case, someone doesn't survive. A life is destroyed. Amy's work was her life and she destroyed that too. That's the main point; it's a lethal encounter. Which way it goes, you can never tell in advance."

"Anyway," Maya continued, "your early theory that Ruth might have killed him for harshly criticizing her book doesn't look that good now, because after her first moment of shock, she agreed with him. Her view is that he did her a favor by persuading her to move on to another project, and that was certainly born out by the books that followed. She rated her Barlow experience at six or seven out of ten. I can't imagine any of the others would give him marks that high."

"And Dina Bauer never struck me as having a skin that was too thin," I said. "Her command of herself was never in question, perhaps because she was in her forties instead of her twenties. I don't think Barlow shook her at all; she knows herself too well, and she was able to filter out what she didn't need, or what flat out made no sense, and use the rest."

"What about Miss Denny?" Maya was looking at Cody as she said this, but I knew she had her own ideas.

"Well, then, Miss Denny." He sighed as he slid his plate to one side and leaned forward on the table. "That's a different story. She travels on the strength of her charm, which is considerable, yet she also has a thick skin, although she doesn't look like it. I've thought about this a lot and I still can't see her killing Barlow."

"Do you know what I think after talking to her?" asked Maya. "I hinted at this before, but we never went into it."

"I'm sure you're going to tell me," he said, "but do I want to hear it?"

"Of course you do. Even though I did like her, I think Miss Denny is a lace collar hard-ass. All those comments of Barlow's in the notebook about her sentimentality missed the point completely. That book she's writing is more like a fantasy version of herself. It's what she would like to be, not what she became after her divorce. Barlow didn't get it at all. Miss Denny should title it, *What I Really Want to Be if I Could Truly Break Loose from my Past.*"

"Barlow's notes don't mention a title," I said.

"You didn't see the manuscript," Cody said to Maya.

"I'm going by what she said to me at the

cocktail party, not that she meant me to take it the way I did. She was trying to impress me with her sincerity and her insights into her personal development, but I can read between the lines. Get the manuscript from Delgado and you'll see what I'm saying."

"He gave them back already, except for the one belonging to Lisa Givens, which he hasn't seen."

"Is he going to help us find her? I'm thinking his office can contact the hotels by phone and get an answer more quickly that we could." We had done this kind of search before on other cases, and it was only by showing up and asking what the room number was that we made any headway.

"He's going to put someone on it. He didn't say when."

"I looked at the Lisa Givens notebook comments again this afternoon," I said. "She has a more cutting edge project than some others. Her lead character wants to be a graphic artist and author. Barlow comes up with the crazy idea that the character, named Carrie, should be a Jane Austen type girl. He goes on in his usual fashion, beating up on Lisa, trying to foist something on her that she never imagined was part of her book."

"And this was going on in Barlow's room at

the Hacienda Old México," said Maya.

"Right, and can you imagine her getting up to go to the bathroom," I said, "and there she sees—remember now, she's a pharmacist—she sees his prescription bottle of Digoxin on that little painted wooden shelf next to the toilet. Lisa can't resist picking it up. She knows exactly what it does, and it gives her a sudden inspiration."

"But how does she get him to take it?" asked Maya.

"She couldn't have, right then," said Cody, "because heart medications usually have an effect that comes on fairly quickly, and this meeting was the afternoon or evening before. I think that Barlow must have taken the Digoxin overdose at breakfast at the earliest, right before he died."

"She wanted him to die giving his speech, to keel over in front of a lot of people, just like he did." I said. "She wanted to humiliate him as well as kill him."

Cody was shaking his head. "I don't know whether she knew enough to think that would happen, but she must've wanted it to be public in some way. Or it could be that there wasn't any chance to give it to him the night before? He had to be ingesting something that she could put it in. She couldn't just hand him ten pills and a glass of water."

"And it wouldn't have been Barlow's own supply that she fed him," I said, "because he might have noticed that many pills missing and gotten alarmed. She could have gotten it anywhere, because here in México, unless it's a narcotic or an antibiotic, no prescription is required. Lisa could walk into any pharmacy and have it in her hand in less than a minute. No record of her buying it would ever be on file. They wouldn't even ask her name."

"Now the question is," said Cody, "where did Justus Barlow have breakfast on the day he died, and was Lisa Givens with him?"

The following morning I called Diego Delgado to ask him how the search was going. I hinted that he needed to talk with Lisa Givens as much as we did. He said that while they had made some enquiries at the obvious places, the bed and breakfasts and hotels that were moderately priced, they hadn't located her. He offered no more than that. I had the impression he was more concerned with another case, so I didn't push him. It had never worked in the past when I had. The only other new information he gave me was that, immediately after the autopsy, Barlow's body had been released from the morgue in Guanajuato and cremated on the instructions of Chad Metcalf, who planned to take the ashes back to New York with him.

An idea had already come to me before this call, since just from the fact that he hadn't called me first, I'd sensed that Delgado was dragging his feet. Whenever he could, he liked to show me he was running a bit ahead of the Zacher Agency, because we were, after all, sometimes his most formidable competition. This new idea involved the possibility that Lisa was staying with someone locally, away from any public accommodations. She could be a person who lived in San Miguel and also attended the conference. It was, I knew from the familiar faces I'd seen, a good draw locally. If that was the case, there might be a record of phone calls from Lisa's room at the Hacienda Old México to this helpful person during the time when she was setting it up. It was likely that Lisa's cell phone from Laramie, Wyoming, would not have coverage this far down into México. I would've gone back to the hotel immediately to check this, but the desk clerk I'd met on my earlier visit hadn't been that welcoming, even in my shattered state, and would probably not be interested in sharing the details of Lisa Givens' bill with me. This meant that our fearless leader would have to get suited up herself and make the visit. She always cleaned up well. One thing I learned long ago is that if you want to get information from a Méxican man, you send an attractive Méxican woman. Male gringos rarely cut it. We're better at strategy than field work.

Beyond that, we each bring a specific type of expertise to the agency. For example, Cody's knowledge of procedure is enhanced by his psychology background. In addition to Maya's management skills, she's always ready to play Mata Hari with a combination of nuance and conviction that few Hollywood hotties could summon to the role. Besides, she clearly enjoys it. She instinctively knows the precise display of cleavage required to launch the conversation on the proper note, and the degree of charm to garnish it with, like curly lettuce around the edges of a salmon mousse. She intuitively understands the clothes and makeup required.

As I watched her walk out the door that morning, wearing her spray-on jean capris and a pale green tank top that made her skin color bloom, I witnessed an extra motion to her hips that I knew was not intended for me, but for the advancement of the agency and the conference.

I also knew in my heart that, like Lola Barker, we each took our job very seriously, and also performed it with several more degrees of finesse than she did.

But my other job is painting, which I'd been neglecting for a while, so after Maya left I went up to the studio and stretched a couple of canvases as if I had a new project in mind. I listened to some of Bill Evans' last recordings as I did this. It led directly to having a couple of ready canvases leaning against the wall, but nothing more.

Maya returned an hour later with three nights worth of discount coupons for the honeymoon suite at the Hacienda Old México, and a single-page phone charge printout.

"Three calls within five hours to the same landline here in town." She read off the number in the breathless tones of a woman who knew she was deeply admired, but was reluctant to say by whom. "I'll call Cody."

Cody had a woman friend in the police department who fed him information from time to time when we didn't want to "bother" Delgado to get it. We only used her when we wanted to fly beneath his radar. In this case, as far as we knew, only the police had access to reverse directory information, where you put in the phone number and out came the owner's name, with his address. This was a perfect task for Cody's admirer. She liked to help, especially since the Zacher Agency had recently been awarded merit certificates after our eighth case, the one we called in our notes, *Identity Crisis*. It gave her a little cover in the event that if she ever got caught helping us, she could argue that her motive was public service.

By midafternoon Cody came over with what we needed, although it wasn't what I expected.

"Barbara Watt?" I said. "Come on, I know her number, and this isn't it."

"I've got her number, too, " Maya said, withoutgrinning.

Cody shrugged. "The police never lie."

"Are you kidding me? The police lie like a rug. Anywhere."

"Now I'm insulted."

"All right. Retired police from Peoria don't lie. For the others, all bets are off."

I hadn't seen Barbara in more than a year, which was a relief to Maya, since Barbara had always shown a keen interest in me that could never be called fraternal. There had been times when I'd had difficulty holding her off, but not recently. I had to admit that my life was more serene in her absence.

"One of us is going to have to talk to her," I said, "if this number is really hers."

"She wouldn't be as open with me," said Maya. "Obviously."

"Or me," said Cody, "for different reasons."

I dialed Barbara's new number. For some reason, Maya and Cody both discreetly left the room.

"*Hola, Chica, como estás?*" I knew Barbara had majored in Spanish.

"Paul, darling! It's been *way* too long." Her voice caressed the receiver.

"What is this number?"

"It's my art studio—you remember it. I've been spending so much time up here that I've been missing calls. I had to put a new line in."

"What are you painting?"

"Still life! They're going great. Why don't you come over and look at them? You know where I am."

"I'd like to. What time is good?"

"This afternoon any time, but you're being way too easy. Is there something else on your mind?"

"Yes, but I'll tell you when I get there."

CHAPTER THIRTEEN

We ate an early lunch, and at 1:30 I drove up alone to the Los Balcones neighborhood to see Barbara Watt. She'd been widowed for several years, since our first case, in fact, but I hadn't seen her much around town lately. She must be thirty now, a tall blonde, blessed with more curves than caution. Like meeting a bus on a steep mountain curve above Oaxaca, you didn't know whether the thrill of encountering her would be survivable. Her vast neocolonial mansion hadn't changed at all. It was still bull's-blood red, and looked freshly painted. The gates were open and I drifted onto the manicured gravel next to her silver Mercedes 600. The houseboy was polishing it, and he ran to the door to let me in.

"I know where the *señora* is," I said to him.

"She expects you, Señor Zacher."

In the foyer I climbed the broad marble

staircase with a feeling of déjà vu. High above, the domed ceiling was lit by a graceful stone cupola with tiny gothic windows on all eight sides. At the top of the stairs I glanced again into the bathroom where Malcolm Brendel had been murdered with an artist's paintbrush. That was our third case. How long ago it seemed now! I had nearly been charged in his death, and Maya and I had hidden in Guanajuato until the smoke cleared. I'm not sure why I thought of them as good times, but they weren't bad to look back on now, after so much more experience. I know they weren't always much fun at the time. But how much more we'd learned since then! I paused to look over the carved balustrade into the great room below. With no special reshuffling of the furniture, it provided seating for thirty people. Beyond, three broad full-length windows looked into the deep garden and over the city. At the far wall of the property, the hillside cascaded down toward *centro*.

At the end of the hall I paused and knocked on the door of the last of the bedrooms, now Barbara's painting studio. When she didn't respond, I pushed it open with no sound. She stood with her smooth back to me, facing the easel, wearing the briefest of cutoff jeans and an old white cotton shirt with the tails tied under her breasts. Her hair was up and knotted with a violet ribbon. Hearing me come in, she set the pallet and brush down and slowly turned around.

"What took you so long, Paul?" Her breathless voice could have belonged to Lauren Bacall addressing Bogey. I liked it. We both admired old movies, and she'd instinctively found the proper note.

"I'm not sure what you mean."

"To call me, I meant. Once you found out I had her."

"You had her?" Barbara was either way ahead of me, or off somewhere on her own script that I lacked a copy of. That was nothing new.

"Lisa Givens. I ran into her at a session of the mystery writing conference, the only one I went to, as it happened. Just luck or a charming coincidence, especially when she told me later over coffee that you were looking for her—she used the word *hunting* and said she wasn't wild about talking to you. You won't be surprised that my first thought was that I might use her to scare something up." She had taken several steps forward as she spoke, and now her blue eyes searched mine from about six inches away. The way her lips articulated each word was something I couldn't ignore. It was more than just pronunciation. "But you're not scared, are you, Paul?"

The last word contained nuances that my

name never had except coming from her mouth.

"A little bit scared, but I'm still holding the panic part at arms length, thank you. I thought we'd finished with this perennial foreplay more than a year ago." She and I had a long history of near misses that had left me feeling either exhilarated or guilty. Usually both.

Her voice took on a more emphatic tone. "This is *never* finished. It's what makes the world go round."

"Your world. It usually spins somewhat faster than mine does."

Her face came into even closer focus as her lips connected with mine. I found my arms around her even before hers went around me. This was familiar terrain indeed, one full of pitfalls and quicksand, and worst of all, exquisite skin. My fingertips were mapping it now on her lower back, and it hadn't changed. "I'm here on a case," I gasped. "This is all about business." I kissed her again.

"Risky business. You just don't know your limits."

I had to agree with her there, as I released her and took a step back. "You haven't changed at all."

"Should I? What would changing be like for me? Or worse, for you? I'm your outside dream. I'm there for you when all else fails. When you've run out of wrong choices, I'm the inevitable winner."

I shook my head, since my thoughts were stumbling over each other. "I can't imagine you any other way. This is changing, though." Eager to deflect the subject, the sweep of my arm took in two walls of paintings, probably twenty-five in total, none of them large in scale. "You've taken off." I stepped closer to inspect a small one. It showed a coffee cup with several upright brushes sticking out of it and three tubes of paint next to it. "I remember this one well." I call this move hiding behind art when reality offers no refuge.

"It's my first picture. That's my point of reference for each new one as I go along."

"I'm proud of what you've done, I really am." Not that I was so proud of what I had done in getting back to this point with her. "There's more progress here than I would ever have imagined. A lot of people start painting and then they peter out when they discover how much more difficult it is than they thought. You ought to find a gallery and start showing. I think you're ready." I felt her arms encircle me from behind like twin snakes from the Garden of Eden, and her breasts pressed against my back. I was ready for the apple at any time. Her lips grazed my neck and her tongue flickered beneath my ear.

"You're way too kind to me," she said. "We'd be good together, even better than you think. But I know, I know, you're still committed to your native girl." She released me and stepped back. Had she seen any of this, Maya would have knifed her by now and felt no remorse.

"So," I said, brightly, turning my back to her paintings. "Where can I find Lisa Givens?" At this point, my voice must have sounded like Ruth Bendickson's.

"She's waiting for you in the library. I told her we might be a while, but I guess I spoke too soon, as usual."

"She's not going to run off? That's what she did last time I saw her."

Barbara shook her head. "I convinced her that you're honest and reasonable, if a little bit too stubborn and principled."

"I call it loyal."

"And you tasted pretty loyal a minute ago."

"Good. I'm glad you sensed I was holding something back. I didn't want to let myself go too much." This was true, in my mind, at least. With both hands on my back, she shoved me firmly out the door and closed it behind me.

Barbara's late husband, Perry, had used a study on the second floor to serve as his office in México. The downstairs library, on the other hand, was a more decorative space off the left front corner of the great room, looking over the narrow end of the garden. Here, I recalled, were kept the old leather bindings, the collector editions, a few antique instruments: one a mahogany and brass telescope on a tripod, another an ancient globe with speculative contours in the region of the Americas. The furniture was Georgian in design and upholstered in leather, with two wing chairs and a piecrust table. The door stood open six inches.

I pushed it open all the way and went in.

"Thanks for not running," I said to Lisa Givens. "I'm Paul Zacher, and this is only a conversation." The brown eyes and sandy blond hair I recognized at once seeing her in the crowd at the conference. Her nose was straight above a sensual mouth. She looked vaguely alarmed, but she wasn't wearing her running shoes, so I thought we could at least make a start.

"I didn't want to talk to you, but I didn't want to give up the rest of the conference, either. When Barbara told me you were coming over, I decided to bite the bullet."

We both sat down, facing each other across the library, which felt intimate after the scale of the great room. Sitting upright with her hands on her knees, Lisa was wearing jeans and a navy cotton tee shirt with an athletic gear logo.

"Thank you. You know that I'm trying to find out who killed Justus Barlow. You also know that you're one of three clients he was seeing here because you saw the manuscripts of the other two when you retrieved yours from his room after he died."

This was a bit forceful, but I didn't know how much time I was going to get with her, and I wanted to shake her loose quickly by making her feel she had to defend herself. It stopped her for only a moment.

"You're not so nice, after all." She folded her arms and settled back further away from me into the camelback sofa.

"If I were nice, Lisa, I'd probably be a florist or an undertaker instead of a detective. This is more about truth than being nice. Please tell me about your relationship with Barlow. I understand he thought you needed help from Jane Austen."

She was wearing no shoes, and pulled one leg up beneath her. She shook her head.

"I couldn't think why he said that. Maybe he told that to everyone? It made no sense, and it convinced me that he didn't have any idea what I was trying to do."

"Others have said that, too. Some thought he was best as a line editor, useful only on detail matters, and that larger concepts were beyond him."

Lisa shrugged and unwound a little. "Telling me to reinvent my main character seemed large enough to me."

"Was she short?"

"Short? No. Why would you say that?"

"I've heard Barlow had a problem with short characters."

"I never saw that."

"I wonder how you came at the writing of fiction, or mysteries, being a pharmacist by background? It must give you a special insight on the chemical means of murder. Perhaps in detection as well."

It crossed my mind that Cody would have asked if I weren't pushing her too hard at this juncture. That she blanched at the question was undeniable. Some blondes, particularly darker blondes, have a darker complexion to match. This was the case with Lisa, and her skin now took on an unhealthy pallor. It was clearly the one thing she was hoping I wasn't going to ask.

"That's why I ran when you saw me."

"I only knew it was you *because* you ran."

"But I knew it was you, and that was enough. I'd seen you at the detective agency talk where everything blew up."

This gave me an unanticipated thought. Placing my elbows on my knees, I leaned forward in a more confidential stance. "There was a time toward the end when the audience surged forward and crowded around our table at the front. Someone we didn't see dropped an important note at the corner where Maya, the woman on our team, was sitting. Did you see who that was?"

Lisa brightened. Here was a way to take the spotlight off herself. "Yes! It was Dina Bauer. She had gone to see Barlow, too. I'd run into her at the Hacienda Old México a couple of days before, and I was sitting with her at your session until everything broke up. I thought leaving that note was an odd thing to do, but she told me earlier that she'd had an idea about Barlow's background. I never knew what it was, but she said she wanted to be sure you got the message. Then, right at that moment, that crazy woman came in from the back and started yelling at everyone. To tell you the truth, I'd forgotten about it until now. I hope that helps you."

Lisa had come over to my side in a way I'd never expected, so I responded in kind.

"I was surprised, although I think I understand why, that you came back and retrieved your manuscript."

"What else could I do? I tried to think about it like a detective. There would be three main suspects, given the three manuscripts. Everyone hated the victim. I mean, even if you got something great from him, you'd still hate him. That's just the way he was. Barlow was a creep!"

"Yet, that's not a capital offense, even in México."

"No." She grew silent, introspective before she spoke again. "I was with him the night—the evening, I mean—before he died. He was horrible, and he ended by asking me to stay for a glass of wine. He even said he wouldn't charge me for it. Do you believe that? He was going to get me drunk so he could seduce me, but he wouldn't even charge me for the wine! What a sweet guy! I went into his bathroom, getting ready to go, and I noticed his meds on a shelf. Naturally, I couldn't help but look at them. They would tell me everything about him. I saw the Digoxin right away."

She put her hands over her face for a

moment, then leaned forward into the space between us.

"I also saw how it could be done. I'd gone around to the pharmacies here, looking at their stock and their procedures, so I knew I could get the Digoxin with no problem."

A loaded silence hung in the air between us for several moments. I could see Lisa Givens reliving that key moment in the bathroom. Suddenly, she shook her head violently. I thought it was denial.

"So you killed him."

She looked at me in shock. "NO! But I knew that I could've done it, and he'd been so horrible about my book, I wanted to do it. Like any writer, I put myself in the position of the killer. That was how it must have happened. It had to be, don't you think?"

"I do think that."

She became more animated. "Well, then I was tortured by it, because the next day, after he died during his speech, I saw myself as the chief suspect, being a pharmacist and knowing what I knew about that drug. His other two clients probably had no idea. I stewed all day about it, and when the last session was over, I ran back to the Old México. In the hallway I found a maid and I gave her a hundred pesos to let me into Barlow's room. I almost choked saying it, but I told her I was his lover. I waited for her to go back down the hall, and then I left with my manuscript under my arm. I was safe! I was home free, until you and I locked glances outside the plot lecture. You can be scary, too, do you know that?"

"That's what Barbara was telling me a little while back. I'll try to reel it in a bit."

I was glad enough to be formidable, but at the same time, I wasn't sure where this left me. Lisa had given me more than I expected, but what I didn't like was that the landscape was now littered with even more suspects who had a strong motive to kill him, and didn't mind talking about it. Each was ready to cheer the killer on his way to trial, as long as it wasn't one of them. For a victim, I preferred the upstanding citizen, one with a long record of public service. Then you knew the motive was unique and concealed. I didn't want a victim that the average crowd could have torn limb from limb without suffering a single regret as they adjourned to the celebratory banquet following his demise.

Lisa Givens was staring at me as if she expected me to release her.

"I don't know what to say to you. As a suspect, you don't look any better or worse to me than the others, but I think you should talk to the police. They're still looking for you, although not as hard as I was, and you need to tell them what you told me. They already know about you slipping in and taking back your manuscript. Just call this man and arrange to come in. He's a decent sort, and I work with him all the time." I wrote Delgado's name and number on a piece of Barbara's monogrammed linen notepaper from the kidney-shaped desk.

"Do you think they'll put me in a cell?"

"No, I don't. But you don't want a hold put on your tourist visa, which could happen if you try to leave the country without talking to them. Delgado knows you're attending the conference, and he also knows it's nearly finished. The police talked to the hotels and bed and breakfasts after you left the Old México, so they're probably thinking you're underground somewhere. They might be expecting to snag you at the Leon airport if you don't turn up before you try to board your plane. They can check what flight you're on too, you know."

After a moment of silence, during which neither of us knew exactly what to say, Lisa stood up and offered me her hand. As I shook it she came closer and kissed my cheek, the standard México greeting or farewell.

"Thank you," she whispered.

"Good luck," I said. I turned and left through the great room.

I considered whether I ought to say good-bye again to Barbara, but I wanted to think about the case, rather than about her. I didn't feel wonderful about Lisa, but neither did I feel a whole lot worse about her than I did about the other suspects. The most telling fact about her was that pharmacy background, but any of them could have looked up Digoxin on the Internet after seeing it in his bathroom. Essentially I was still running in place.

I dialed Maya as I drove down Santo Domingo.

"Nothing remarkable about Lisa," I said. "She could have done it, but I'm not ready to turn her over to the vigilantes. Barbara asked about you, by the way. I said we were still together and doing fine. If you've got time, I'd like to do a walk down the Ancha and see if we can find out where Barlow had breakfast that last morning, and with what lovely companion. It's a long shot, but we might get something. I'll meet you at the bottom of Codo in a little bit."

She said she'd get Cody involved if he was available.

CHAPTER FOURTEEN

Ancha de San Antonio has no shortage of restaurants within easy walking distance of both the Hacienda Old México and the Rosewood, but most of them don't serve breakfast. After the three of us met at the Codo intersection, we separated to check them out. We were hampered by having no picture of Lisa Givens, although we did have a good head and shoulders shot of Justus Barlow from the conference brochure. It was good in the sense that it made him look benign and presentable, as well as ten years younger, so the resemblance was approximately accurate, but still misleading in some important ways.

I started at the restaurant of the Hacienda Old México and got nothing. A couple people recalled seeing Barlow in the lobby, but I found no one who'd observed him having breakfast with a woman, or even alone.

Farther down the street, I checked in Siempre Desayuno and got a little less. It's a small dark place inside, with an outdoor courtyard too close to the Ancha traffic, and therefore too noisy to carry on a reasonable conversation. I also thought it was too public. "He's short," I said, "and he walks with a limp. One shoe is altered to help him with balance. I'm wondering if he had breakfast here three days ago. He may have been with a woman."

I got the Méxican shrug, which in this case meant that he may have, but she wouldn't tell me, or that he hadn't, and it was none of my business. Or yet again, she wasn't working on the day in question. Or five other things, none of them any more likely or helpful. I thanked her profusely—there was no sense in both of us being rude, and she hadn't been, only unhelpful.

Approximately at the intersection of Nemesio Diez, the street of the Rosewood, I went into Café Monet, a place I enjoy for breakfast now and then. I hadn't seen Maya or Cody up on Zacateros, but they couldn't be that far away. The Monet has a living room atmosphere with big chairs and a lot of art on the walls that changes every six weeks or so. It's all for sale. Each table is different, suggesting a setting that's been furnished over a period of years, heavily dependent on garage and estate sales. Most of all, it speaks of comfort, and invites intimate conversations. If I had a girlfriend, I'd take her there, and I have—Maya loves it. Although it was hard to imagine after what she'd said, if Lisa Givens had arranged a morning meeting with Justus Barlow in order to poison him, I could also see it happening there. He would never have expected it was his final meal. Maybe she had promised to bring him some money to settle her account.

People at two tables waved to me as I came in, but I only waved back without stopping. I wasn't up for a casual conversation that could go on and on. The owner wasn't present, so I talked to a waiter named Chucho, who seemed to be in charge. I showed him Barlow's photo and described him. In response, a knowing grin came over his face and he did a little limping dance that I thought was unkind, but there you were. Maybe Barlow hadn't tipped him enough, or at all.

Next I tried to describe Lisa Givens. I knew her appearance much better after our conversation, and I listed her mannerisms as well as her blond hair, height, brown eyes and other physical traits. Chucho shook his head.

"No, that was not her with him, *señor*. The

woman with the man you are searching for is very tall, much taller even than you. She is not young, maybe almost sixty, and she has a voice like a whistle, squeaky and high. Her hair is dyed the color of sand, and thin. It is teased out to seem thicker." Here he smiled. "My wife does hair. They sat there." He pointed at a table in the back, distant from the others, and more private.

I was so startled I couldn't think of anything else to say. In my mind, Ruth Bendickson had no longer been a suspect after her conversation with Maya.

"Do you want to know what they ate that morning, señor? I can get the ticket for you."

"No. No, I don't. Did you see her touch his coffee? Did she put anything in it?"

"No, *señor*. But I was not looking at them much because I was working five other tables."

"That's all, then. Thank you, Chucho. Wait—were they friendly with each other? Laughing or joking like old friends? What was their mood?"

"Oh no, they were very serious the whole time. The woman looked angry."

I gave him fifty pesos and my thanks before I left with a hollow space in my stomach and the sense that I'd misread most of this case. On the other hand, you misread most cases until you came to a point where you didn't, and then they were solved, so it was nothing different.

When I paused on the sidewalk in front of Café Monet, a cab pulled over hopefully, but I waved it off. Maya had said that Ruth Bendickson told her she hadn't seen Barlow in six years. Yet what could be more natural than that Ruth and Justus should have breakfast together to reconnect on the first day of the conference? They had known each other well in the days of Ruth's ill-fated first book. Even more, they would surely have found much to talk about in her subsequent success, which he had helped her launch by convincing her to drop *These Things Are Mine*. I could think of only one reason she had denied seeing Barlow: Ruth had known he was going to die later that morning.

But, if she had killed him, what was her motive? I had to admit I knew practically nothing about her. I'd never even spoken to her at the cocktail party. I'd never read a single word she'd written. Was she ironic in her work? Was she overbearing and too clever? I could believe that. Aside from being the tallest woman I'd ever seen, I had noticed that she was reserved, but not extremely so. Why wouldn't she be reserved in a crowd of people she didn't know, all of whom were focused on everything she said. Writers,

I assumed, worked mostly in private, and that's how they organized their thoughts. That had been the case with Maya. They wouldn't necessarily be relaxed in a crowd of people waiting for them to say one clever thing after another, gemlike tidbits that were equal to the best of their writing. Maybe some people in the crowd were even secretly taping her remarks.

I noticed Maya and Cody approaching as they walked down Zacateros. Maya was shaking her head when they reached me.

"Nothing. No one saw them."

"They could've taken a cab across town, for that matter," Cody said. "They could have left the neighborhood. It would have made more sense."

I said nothing.

"Let's go back up to the Rosewood and check there," Maya continued, "although that seems less likely because it would be so public. A lot of the conference people would've seen them." Looking at me, she must have noticed something odd in my expression. "What? Did you find out something?"

I nodded slowly. "It was Ruth, not Lisa Givens. The waiter at Café Monet remembered them. Barlow had breakfast with her there the morning he died. They sat at that table way in the back, the one that's always so dark."

"I know the one," said Cody. "It would be dark enough to drop something in his coffee if he got up to go to the bathroom."

"I can hardly believe that!" said Maya, wide-eyed.

Cody was shaking his head. "It's not enough, though, Paul. Just because the waiter saw them together doesn't prove she poisoned him, only that she could have. The defense could come up with fifty other people who also saw him in that time frame. Unless the waiter actually saw her put something in his coffee or juice?"

"No. I asked him that."

"Then we've got no case. We've got her for opportunity, and that's it. No means, no motive. Worse, there are no witnesses to anything meaningful, and no physical evidence of any kind. If placing them together at Café Monet is the solution to this case, we can kiss any resolution goodbye. Chad Metcalf probably won't even pay on that much."

"Besides," said Maya, with a distressed look, "she's an internationally known and respected writer. We'd be laughed out of this business. I can't understand why she'd do it. Why would she need to?"

We started walking back home. I guess it wasn't the first case we've had where we thought we knew the criminal but couldn't prove the deed.

"I suppose I should be the one to tell Chad Metcalf," Maya said.

"Normally, since you're the head of the agency. In this case, though, I don't think we should tell him anything yet. After all, we can't prove it. It would only be an accusation, one that he doesn't want to hear. He'll deny it before we can finish the story, and then, with his bizarre staff, word will leak out and we'll never have a chance to nail her. I think Chad Metcalf has trouble working in his own interest, and I don't want to help him demonstrate that again."

"Would he break a confidence like that?" asked Cody.

"I don't know what he'd do, but his first thought would be how to spin it. Who knows where that would go? Our only chance to wrap this up is to keep Ruth from knowing what we've discovered."

That night Maya was still restless when we went to bed. She hadn't said much more about the case as we shared a cognac on our roof terrace at sunset. I thought she was avoiding it because it had taken such a disturbing turn. Sometimes we only wanted to take a break from constantly going over the evidence, since a case can start to consume your mind in unhelpful ways. Whatever the reason, I knew she was still upset that it looked like Ruth had killed Barlow. Was she assuming that people who could write well about fictional crime were inherently good people because they were good writers? It didn't seem the time to bring it up. Maybe in the harsh light of day, during breakfast, when we usually talked about hard-edged things: the utility bills, renewing the license plates on the new van, which were so damn expensive merely because it was new. How it was time to get the six-month emission sticker again, and how it was cheaper to be poor, but not as much fun.

"I still can't understand why she would do it." Maya opened and then closed her book without looking inside at the text. "I know I've said that about five times now, but she is so far above him. Killing that worm gains her nothing that I can see."

"That you can see. That's the point. We can't see the motive, but it's there anyway. It's right in front of us, somehow, and we've got to dig it out."

"I've read a lot of mysteries."

"I know. And most of them are twisted, right? Unlike the motives we normally see in our cases, which have usually been simple. Greed, revenge."

"Lust. I'm thinking of Jack and Jill here."

"There aren't that many capital sins," I said. "We could use a few more, they can be pretty interesting."

"Do you think this could be partly about bringing her down? Is she a target because she's so successful? Could someone be framing her because of that? She has breakfast with Barlow after not seeing him in years, and then maybe someone else kills him. Is that why we can't find any motive for her to do it? Tell me, because I like her, and I want her to be innocent, even though she was a little stiff at times. And at the interview I didn't feel she was holding back anything evil. I thought that what she said was true, mostly. Maybe she lied about seeing Barlow again just because he was killed and she didn't want to be a suspect, but the rest was believable. The conversation even had some depth that I didn't expect from her."

"Maybe the most convincing lie is one wrapped in the truth, so it's delivered in that context of believability. But this isn't about bringing Ruth Bendickson down. I think this case is a tragedy. When I found out it was Ruth having breakfast with Barlow at Monet, and not Lisa, I was speechless. I don't begrudge Ruth her success, and I don't wish her any ill. I've never even spoken to her. You know how I am, I just go where the case leads me."

"But if this is how it ends, I don't *like* it."

"I know, but you rarely do." I pulled her over against my chest and lifted the hair off her face. "They never go where you want them to go—the easy, nasty villain, the killer you can spot a mile away whose capture and conviction causes the crowd to cheer. Then we all go home feeling great, knock back a good cognac, and hit the sheets with no regrets, sleeping like babies after a little fooling around. But sometimes the killer is also the hero, and that's not so easy to handle. Ask Cody. I know he's been there before, and more than once."

"Then this is too much like real life. I specifically wouldn't ask him for that reason. Having some illusions can be good, don't you think? It's like believing your boyfriend never slept with anyone else before you."

There was no answer to this, good or bad. I didn't say that sometimes it's the victim or the client who's nasty, and the killer may be worthy of our respect in many ways. I couldn't feel Maya's eyes close against my shoulder, but after a few minutes, I sensed from her even breathing that they had. My own followed shortly. I can't say I went to sleep with relief, but certainly I had no regrets about moving on.

If Barlow's notebook was like other pieces of evidence on some of our cases, its value evolved as events progressed, as we developed more of a matrix to set its individual parts against. I spent some time with those pages again the next morning, going over in detail the chapters that dealt with our suspects, and with Amy Wendt, whose role beckoned to us, but we still didn't grasp. Dina Bauer's instincts had prompted her to bring that part to our attention again at our disastrous meeting. I had tried to reach her again and couldn't. More than that, parts of the notebook that hadn't meant anything earlier might now be highly relevant. It was mostly mental grunt work, but that was what sustained the business, and it often paid off. Maya wasn't up yet, and I sat out on the loggia with my coffee. This far into March the weather already felt like summer, and the mornings were fresh but mild. When I settled at the table, the grackles were already in place working the bamboo, running through their tropical bird imitations. They are the most versatile mimics in this part of the avian world.

I also had Maya's and Cody's notes for comparison, and I studied them in detail before I took up the notebook again. Now that Ruth Bendickson was our principal suspect, for the first time I paid particular attention to Barlow's notes on her sessions, and compared them to Maya's reconstruction of her interview. I could see why Maya thought Ruth was forthcoming, but to me, knowing what we now knew, it looked more like using a lot of truth to conceal some important lies. Since one lie we had caught already was about dates—that Ruth hadn't seen Barlow since she'd worked with him years before—I wondered whether there were other dates that she had also adjusted to support her own version of the facts. Trends can matter in these cases; the past points the way to the future.

One important feature of Maya's interview with Ruth was the character of the older writer's intersection with Amy Wendt, because she was the only one we knew who could comment on Amy, aside from her brother Michael. Yes, Ruth said she had met Amy twice at Barlow's office. Office, I thought? What would he have had in New York, with the peanuts he was making? It didn't matter now. But

Ruth also stated that she and Barlow were finished with their work before the time when Amy killed herself. She'd claimed she heard about Amy's death from someone on the faculty at Bolton College, but she'd never mentioned who that was. Could it be because it was information that could be checked?

At this point I went back into the notebook. The block capital note in Amy's file that trumpeted her death was dated June 14. Flipping ahead into Ruth's pages, the entry for her last visit was July 5, three weeks later. So Barlow had not only known about Amy's death before Ruth left, but it angered him because he wouldn't get paid. He would probably have said something to Ruth, since they had a better relationship than he had with most of his clients, maybe with all of them. I was willing to bet that Ruth heard about it in detail from Barlow, and more than once.

So why would she lie about this too? As an investigator, I know that lies can be as revealing as the truth, since they tell you what the speaker wants you to believe. The truth is usually the opposite. Every statement, whether true or false, contains information of one kind or another; so reading it correctly is the key.

I rarely get a great insight, except in painting, and the Zacher Agency doesn't often depend on them, because they are as rare as fresh tortillas in Nova Scotia. Yet, I suddenly saw again the pile of three battered manuscripts on Barlow's tacky veneered desk at Hacienda Old México on the day he died. The inevitable question that followed was what had happened to Amy Wendt's two manuscripts at her death? Coffee stained, the title page dotted with the blotchy grease of donuts, powdered inside with spider webs and bird feathers, scrawled with the incomprehensible penciled squiggles of the book doctor's testy emissions? In her notebook pages, Barlow had made no mention of the disposition of Amy's manuscripts. Had he forgotten them as quickly as he forgot Amy herself once she could no longer pay?

Michael Wendt had told Cody that his sister destroyed everything before she killed herself. Her computer files were intentionally erased by her own hand. The machine itself was recycled, her important life's work vaporized. Her body interred. She was utterly silenced.

I was staring at the waxy blooms on the bromeliads thinking about this when Maya appeared, pulling her hair together at the back of her head. She bent over and kissed me on the forehead. I went into the kitchen and poured her a cup of coffee.

"Have you solved it yet?" she asked. "This is usually when you do it, if you're going to. I wake up alone in bed and I think, 'He's on it!'"

"I'm still where we were with it last night. Ruth did it but we can't prove it. I've got a question for you. Take Ruth's three books—didn't you say the last one was the weakest of the group?"

"That happens, I guess. I'll find out when I get to my own third one." She stifled a yawn and took a sip of the coffee. "Usually it's the second one that doesn't cut it. In the publishing business they call it the 'sophomore slump.'"

"Did you notice that weakness yourself when you read them, or was it mainly from what the critics said?"

"Well, this is what I thought: to me the second one was easily the equal of the first, but the third one lacked passion. It even felt a little self-conscious. In the first two books Rachel, her main character, was enthusiastic and often wild at times. She was always exciting, and she swept you along even when she was being a little foolish. That was part of her charm. She could take chances without thinking about the possible consequences. You still believed in her because you sensed that she was a winner and her instincts were right. But in the third book, while Rachel

THE BOOK DOCTOR

still had some of that, it felt like she acted as if she had more to lose. She seemed *older* and less bold, as if she was holding back. One review I read recognized that too, but the critic said it was because Rachel had gotten a reputation as a crime solver and she had to protect it."

"Did you agree with that?"

"No. I understood the comment, but I thought it was more than that. To me it felt like Ruth was running out of gas on the series, and was starting to imitate herself, like some people do in painting. You don't, I know, but you do see it, and we've talked about it at gallery openings. Maybe she'd only had enough energy or inspiration for two of the books, but she had to write the third one because it had been presented as a trilogy and she felt committed. Maybe she'd signed a three-book contract, so she was locked in. Besides, they sold so well that she would have been tempted by the money in any case, even if she sensed herself that the third one was the weakest. What are you thinking?"

"Well, this is from way out in left field, but what if Ruth really didn't write..."

"Oh my god!" Maya jumped up so abruptly that her wicker chair fell over. "You're thinking the first two are Amy Wendt's missing books!"

263

I nodded. "Right, and Ruth wrote only the third one herself, but she couldn't pull it off on the same level."

"But Amy was still alive when Ruth finished with Barlow. That's what she told me."

I pushed the copied notebook pages toward her. "Not according to Barlow's notes at the time. Ruth finished with him three weeks *after* Amy killed herself. If in frustration he had just shoved her manuscripts into a pile in a closet, Ruth could've walked away with them. Maybe she stuck them in her satchel while Barlow was down the hall in the bathroom. Particularly if he'd told her about them earlier, it might have given her an idea when Amy died. She told you that she didn't use Barlow at all on *Rachel's Folly*, didn't she?"

"She did, and now I see why. She said she'd learned everything she needed from him."

"That's right, in a way. I think she learned that Amy had left some good stuff behind, and at that point, Barlow had the only copies of it in existence, even though he didn't know it."

"But why wouldn't Michael Wendt have asked for them back?" she asked.

"He wouldn't if he believed Amy had destroyed everything. He might have thought she'd already taken them back herself and disposed of them. She could have told him directly she'd destroyed it all. If she misled her brother about what she'd left at Barlow's office, maybe it was because she couldn't stand the thought of seeing him again to retrieve them. Maybe she knew he wouldn't give them to her unless she paid him. And what would her mental state have been anyway? Was there a lot of clear thinking at that point? To do what she did, she was clearly deep ended. Or, if Barlow had pounded her into submission, she may have thought the books were worthless, so it didn't matter if he still had those manuscript copies. They were going nowhere, and so was she."

"We'll have to verify parts of that. We can have Cody call Michael again."

"Then the other question," I said, "was why Barlow didn't catch up with Ruth when those books were published. Maybe he wasn't a reader? What if he spent all his time editing very rough drafts of books that needed a lot of work. Then for recreation he did quilting or watched television, and he couldn't stand to read anything else."

"Something like that," she said. "It could be like being a plumber. You don't come home from work and fix your own toilet for fun."

CHAPTER FIFTEEN

Cody came by that evening after he'd talked to Michael Wendt again. We'd briefed him by phone that afternoon on why I'd concluded that Ruth had stolen Amy's books. I asked him not to mention my theory to Michael.

"It's about what we thought," Cody said. "Michael told me that at the end she was increasingly irrational, mumbling about the uselessness of everything, having bouts of temper verging on rage. Then she disappeared from the house without saying where she was going. There was no goodbye. Two days later, after Michael had been calling everybody they knew, her body was found by a maid in a cheap motel room in Hoboken. An empty pill bottle and a drained liter of cheap vodka were at the side of her bed. Her laptop was on the desk, still running, and all the files relating to her books were erased with that function that makes them irrecoverable. Michael tried. He took it to a Mac expert, and it was impossible to get them back."

"Did she leave a note?" Maya asked.

Cody looked at his notes. "Yes, it was only four words. 'Everything is gone now.' I asked him if she'd ever threatened to kill herself before, and he said no, but she'd once said to him that if anything ever happened to her, he should destroy all of her writing."

"Did he remember the titles of her books?" Maya asked quietly.

"Only that they both started with the main character's name, Rebecca. He said they were like *Rebecca's something*, and *Rebecca's something else.* That's all he remembered. There had been three fragments of early printed drafts in the house they shared, but Michael couldn't find them when he went through Amy's belongings after she died."

"Then I can guess what the titles really were," Maya said. *"Rebecca's Folly* and *Rebecca's Loves.* So I think we finally have a motive. Barlow must have eventually realized what happened to the manuscripts Amy left with him."

"And he decided to collect from Ruth," I added. "Maybe he'd been furnished an advance copy of the conference brochure to check that his own information was correct, and he saw Ruth there too, author of her two Rachel books that were so similar in title to Amy's. He goes back to check on them and can't find the manuscripts in his pile. He remembers that Ruth moved on shortly after Amy's death and didn't use him for her next book. He always must have wondered why. After all, he was so damn good. Bingo."

"Then his fortune is suddenly made," said Cody. "Although his fate is sealed at the same time, thinking he can now blackmail Ruth and hit the jackpot. Once he got down here and called her for a meeting, she would've guessed from his tone what had to be coming. She must have been expecting this for years, and she knew what she had to do."

"She told me she remembered that he had a heart condition," said Maya.

"We still can't prove a thing," I said. "Even with a motive, we're only one step better than we were before. We've got no witnesses and no physical evidence."

"We can start combing the pharmacies to see if anyone remembers her."

"What if she phoned it in and sent someone else after it? That's easy to do," said Maya. "Most of the pharmacists here have someone who speaks

English."

"If you need this medication," said Cody, "you might be too shaky to come in for it yourself. That's your excuse for using a messenger."

"There are only two days left in the conference," I said. "Then Ruth is gone back to the U.S., and Delgado will never be able to get her extradited back down here to face a murder charge. I think our only chance is to set her up."

With no more discussion I dialed the conference reception desk at the Rosewood. They'd been told to supply us with any guest or staff information we needed. I asked for Ruth Bendickson's number out at the Wilson house in el Cortijo. In a moment she picked it up.

"Hello? Who is this please?"

I hadn't spoken with her before, but I remembered the oddly shrill, quavering voice from when I stood at the edge of the crowd at the cocktail reception. Ruth didn't know me, and even if she had glanced my way that evening, I doubted she would ever remember me. That night there must have been between 150 and 200 people present that she had never seen before, and I hadn't come within thirty feet of her. What I was about to do couldn't have been done by Cody. Being her same height, she might easily have picked him out of the crowd that night. Maya, of course, she'd recall from their interview. I was the only one of the right age and gender. Face to face, she would never know who I was.

"My name is Michael Wendt," I said to Ruth Bendickson. "Amy was my sister. I think we need to have a serious talk tomorrow, because I know what you did."

CHAPTER SIXTEEN

Rather than take the elevator the next morning, I chose to walk the three flights of steps up to the Rosewood's rooftop bar. The journey was a brief space to compose myself in, to try to prepare for the drama I was about to unleash. On the phone I'd given Ruth enough information so she'd be able to prepare a strategy in advance. Her reaction might well be outrage; what kind of person was I to accuse a notable author like her of plagiarism or outright theft? Or she might choose an unequivocal denial. It was true that I couldn't prove the accusation, and I had no identification showing I was Michael Wendt. I could hardly say I'd forgotten my wallet. This conversation might last for only a single sentence. Or perhaps Ruth was a businesswoman at heart and she'd offer a deal we could both live with. On the other hand, most academics I'd known didn't usually have much of a head for business and no tolerance for people who challenged their authority.

Or might she break down and confess imme-diately, offering restitution in exchange for secrecy? That was the most unlikely option. She didn't look like a person who would easily cave.

I came out blinking into the blazing sunlight of the rooftop. The long bar ran along the interior side, its back to the courtyard far below. Low tables lined the outer parapet, which was a waist-high wall with an eight-inch cast iron gallery rail mounted on it. Beyond, the city rolled over the hills and through the valleys in a panoramic display. The Parroquia, the church at the plaza, with its pink and gray spires, was the featured monument in the center of a perfect picture postcard of old México.

I was surprised to find Ruth already seated at a small table near the center of the rail. The bar-tender was the only other person present. I was five minutes early. She obviously thought this meeting important, which didn't argue for her innocence. She hadn't ordered yet and she rose when I approached. I didn't have to pretend I wasn't nervous, because even if I really had been Michael Wendt, I'd still have been nervous.

"Sit down," she said with no visible courtesy.

"Thanks for meeting me." We both sat down.

"I hardly had a choice. What do you have to substantiate your story? Which is preposterous, by the way."

Interesting, I thought, because I hadn't said what the story was. From my shirt pocket I removed a small memory stick. It was seven or eight years old, a Chinese-made SanDisk I used to store older backups of tax records and photos of my paintings. It was only 500 megs and looked suitably well-used, although I hadn't added anything to it in a couple of years. I set it on edge on the table in front of me within easy grasp and slid it back and forth a couple of times on the cloth. At that moment the waiter came over and we both ordered *café Americano*.

"That could be anything," Ruth said with a shrug, after he left. "It's probably your laundry list." She pronounced it londry, and looked bored already.

"Maybe. But there's also room on it for the two books my sister wrote. And a lot more that she might have written, had she lived. One of them is titled *Rebecca's Folly*, and the other is *Rebecca's Loves*. Notice that I didn't say Rachel, like in your books. That came later, when you went through and changed every instance of the main character's first name as you retyped Amy's paper manuscripts. By that time, they had the usual scruffy appearance of everything

Barlow touched. Then you got them published as your own. If you look at these two files, you'll find that the last date when either of them was changed was June 7, more than five years ago. That was the week before Amy killed herself."

When Ruth realized that I knew the titles of Amy's books and the date of her death, the balance quickly shifted between us. She looked like she had discovered herself clawing at something slippery, and stared at the memory stick as if it contained her own death sentence. The waiter returned with our order, and Ruth sipped her coffee silently, now turning away to look past the edge of the parapet. "Those books are my work." She plucked absently at the top button of her blue cotton shirt.

I heard no stress in her voice, only certainty.

"How can you say that? I suppose you took out a few adverbs, besides changing the names. Did that make them yours? I think you were merely the *stenographer*—hardly enough to get you on Oprah."

Ruth sighed and looked off toward the Parroquia. She appeared to be considering her position before she turned to face me.

"I know you think you're being awfully clever, Mr. Wendt, and I can't say that I blame you. But let's be honest here; your sister killed herself. No one else made her take those pills, not even Justus, no matter how nasty he was to her. When she took her own life, Amy's books were *abandoned*; that's the governing word here, can you see that? She may even have thought all the copies were destroyed. From what I heard, that was certainly her intent. But she was sloppy in that as in other things. I'm actually not surprised you found that file. If she left the manuscripts at Justus's office for me, or anyone to find, why not these copies on that stick somewhere else?"

She waited for this to sink in, but I didn't respond. I hadn't thought of her taking this argument, almost one of outright ownership. The waiter returned and refreshed our coffee.

"Amy said in her note that everything was destroyed."

"But she was obviously mistaken, wasn't she? What was so wrong with me taking them," Ruth continued, after he moved out of earshot, "when they could never have done her any good? You must realize that, unlike what everyone thinks, this business is not only about writing books; in fact, it's very far from that. It's about making the whole process happen: the publicity, the promotion, the public appearances, the glad-handing, the autographs and interviews. It's about attending conferences like this when it turns your stomach. Your sister was a damaged person who was never capable of doing *any* of this, according to what I heard from Justus. I believe you couldn't disagree with that. She would've quickly broken down in the process, even if she'd gotten that far. The publishing world is a nasty place, Mr. Wendt, full of fraud and false gurus. Full of phony advice from people who little know what they're talking about, but are quite knowledgeable about trading on your dreams—that's their only skill. Your sister would've wilted on her first day out in public."

While I knew now my theory about Ruth was right, at least as far as the manuscripts went, I wasn't ready yet to tackle the ethical nuances of what she had done. That could wait a little.

"Amy left this in her makeup case," I said, holding up the stick. I had rehearsed this last night. "She had acted to destroy all the big things she loved, so you can understand why I could never bring myself to get rid of the small items she left behind. Even though they had no real significance, nothing else was left of her, so I couldn't remove them. I was shocked to find this in a side pocket next to her eyelash curler."

"I can well imagine, after what went before. You believed, like everyone, I suppose, that both the books were gone."

Ruth's voice was not hostile. I almost felt she was putting herself in my place. Was this empathy coming from the writer in her? The function where she could put herself in anyone's head, even mine in this situation? Was I now a character in one of her books—the villain? I set the stick down again, just out of her reach. It was like a baton, a way of directing the conversation.

"Did you think this would never come out? How did you keep Barlow quiet all these years?" She made a useless gesture. "I don't think that fool ever knew I took those manuscripts. He hated mysteries, and you'll think this odd, as coarse as he was, but he always read poetry for enjoyment. He liked e. e. cummings, T. S. Elliot."

"So it turns out that Barlow was a kind and sensitive soul," I said, with no change of expression. "I still hold him partly responsible for Amy's death."

"Inward is the way I thought of him. He rarely looked outside himself, and perhaps he wasn't capable of it. Anyway, I understood that about him, and I took a chance because I thought the stakes were so high. I knew someone in New York who would snap those books up."

"Didn't Barlow realize what Amy had?"

"If he did, he still thought he needed to beat on her the way he did nearly everyone who came to him. Perhaps he needed to get that out of the way first. But when he talked about her to me, I was intrigued. Then when she committed suicide, I saw my chance. Of course, it bothered me at night, when I couldn't sleep, not what I'd done, because I owed her nothing, but that I could be caught at any time. Especially when *Rachel's Folly* was so successful, all I could think about was the truth coming out. But as the years passed one after another, I began to feel safer. I dreamed of the future I have mostly had, until you called me last night."

"But you were never totally safe." I allowed my voice to sound sympathetic.

"No. The image I always had was of him moving his tiny office, and having to clear out the first drafts and old copies of manuscripts he'd worked on. Justus was a pack rat; he could never throw anything away, not that he knew what he had. Those stacks and piles were the accumulated substance of his credentials. I saw him suddenly stand upright, having gone through all of them one day, and realize that your sister's two books were no longer there."

"Would he then have guessed where they were?"

Ruth took a long sip of her coffee. "Eventually. He wasn't stupid, only insensitive and short-sighted."

The waiter came over and refilled our coffee cups again. He was a strange intrusion into an unworldly story. I waited until he moved off before I spoke.

"You were fortunate, getting by with it all this time."

"More than I deserved, perhaps." She turned and leaned toward me. "But those books are mine now. They gave me what I had always dreamed of. You have not, I assume, been at the conference here."

"No. Looking for your name on the Internet, I saw it advertised, which is how I knew you were featured. I got on a plane."

"When you leave, then, look around as you're going down through this hotel. Look at all the people who want to write and can't, or can write a little, and then stumble and go no farther. I see how they look at me, how they long to touch my hand. They thrust their copies of my book at me to autograph. Whenever they open the cover they'll see that page first and they'll think of that moment. With their index fingers they will trace the ink of my signature."

"Your name on Amy Wendt's books," I said.

"They were Amy's until her death, but not after, Mr. Wendt. I know you'll advocate for the rights of inheritance, that's your natural position, but it's a mere legality. I see a more obvious imperative here. Just as a piece of bread belongs more certainly to a starving man than to a glutton, no matter which of them grasps it in his hand, those books belong to *me*. I needed them more than your sister did—she proved that the day she took her own life. They have made me what I am, what I wanted to be from childhood. Those two books contained my essence. Without them, I'd be downstairs now, sitting in the audience while some third-rate hack rambles on about self-publishing to people who will never finish their first book." Ruth pressed the tip of her index finger into the top of the table as if she would push it all the way through. "Make no mistake about this: there are dreamers, and there are people who seize the day. That's all that matters in this life. You know which one I am."

She waited for me to respond, but I had nothing ready for this. I didn't want to say how much I understood it and was almost inclined to agree with it, so I remained silent as she went on. "Had you been able to get them published after your sister's death, and effectively promoted them, as if you ever could, what would they have given you beyond greater prosperity? Would they have made you what you had always needed to be for your entire life?"

I could only shake my head. I knew I was talking to someone who had struggled as I had. She nodded as if she'd made her point.

"What do you do for a living, Mr. Wendt?"

"I'm a machinist." I plucked this right out of the air.

"A worker in metals, then, but not in words."

"Yes."

"My point is made. Even correctly promoted and successful, those books would have brought you nothing but money, which is the smallest part of the reward."

I was almost starting to believe Ruth had more right to the books than Michael Wendt did, but there was still the matter of Barlow's murder. My experience had been that crimes were like potato chips; one led to another. If she could argue plausibly for the book theft, it didn't mean she also had a pass to murder Justus Barlow, no matter how hateful he was.

"That's an interesting argument," I said, "but perhaps it's now my turn to seize the day. I understand why you think you have a right to Amy's books, but as you suggest, the law defines the claim I have as her heir, even without a will. I'll make you an offer. With Barlow gone and my interest settled out, you'll be able to sleep at night, and so will I."

I couldn't read the smile she gave me. It wasn't warm, nor was it ironic. Perhaps it was only meant to encourage me to continue. I had already thought in detail about what I planned to say next.

"My guess is that you've made about three million dollars from the first two books. I've seen the sales figures. Let's say that taxes and your agent's commissions took half of that. You've got 1.5 million left, and the third book is selling well, even if it's not up to Amy's work. I could sue you and we'd both be tied up in court for a long time. There might also be criminal charges coming out of it, at least for fraud. It's hard to know how much I'd walk away with, but the lawyers would get rich off both of us. That's a certainty. I'll settle for half a million, and for that you get this stick and my release of any interest in Amy's books. I'll also guarantee confidentiality. You'll keep your reputation. We would both be able to go on with our lives. That's worth something as well."

I watched a variety of responses contending in her expression. Of course, if she agreed to this, I'd fall right on my face. But I didn't think she would. I had also intentionally omitted any mention of a murder charge in the Barlow case, or even that it was suspected that she'd killed him. When she didn't answer, I added, "It leaves you in great shape, if not entirely whole, and leaves me feeling better than I do now, especially once I pay off my mortgage. Consider that your third book is selling well partly on the strength of Amy's work too. I don't ask for any of that money. There could even be more in the pipeline, if you can manage to write more. You have a great deal of momentum now."

"Let me think for a moment," she said, covering the lower part of her face with one hand as she looked out over the parapet.

Leaning back in my chair, I raised my hands to my head and smoothed my hair on both sides. This was the signal we'd agreed upon for the bartender to walk over and tap me on the shoulder.

"You are Señor Michael Wendt?"

I nodded.

"I have a phone call for you from the reception. You can take it at the bar if you wish."

I excused myself, picked up the memory stick, slid it into my shirt pocket, and followed him back to the bar. Keeping my back to Ruth, I walked in an unhurried fashion, but I was nervous enough to stumble. Lifting the phone and holding it to my ear,

I listened to a dial tone while I nodded occasionally as I looked over the bar down into the central court-yard and mouthed a few words. The bartender, who had been replaced before our arrival by Delgado's associate, Officer Hugo Peña, mopped the bar surface, watching my table at an oblique angle through his sunglasses. From the angle of his head, he might have been scanning something at the far end of the bar.

"It is done, señor," he said softly, after another moment, as he bent over to place the sponge under the bar. This meant Ruth Bendickson had put some-thing in my coffee. After a few more seconds had passed, I hung up the phone, turned and thanked him, and walked back to the table. I couldn't have said how my face must have looked.

It gave me a queer sensation to know that my cup contained what was most likely a fatal dose of Digoxin. We had Ruth now; she had repeated her crime as we thought she might. It gave me no sat-isfaction whatever to be right. She had articulated her dilemma too clearly, too forcefully, for me to be unsympathetic, even though she'd tried to kill me af-terwards. My life since the age of sixteen had been driven by a creative ambition too. I have the skill and the perseverance to be a successful painter. If not a great one, I am at least one capable of making a respectable living in a field where most fail to find an audience. Without that, I would have had what Ruth depicted as her own situation before Amy's books—a life lived without the possibility of ever developing real meaning.

Knowing what she had done, I sat down and looked her in the eye. She was my murderer, and she stared back at me without blinking. After years of enormous success, victory came easily to her, and she bore it with a practiced grace I could only admire, particularly at that moment.

Of course, we all choose what will give meaning to our lives. For some, it's parenthood, followed by grandparenthood. For others, it's being a spectator of team sports, or pursuing the lonely and silent specter of God. These are easily fulfilled. For others, it's making large amounts of money. This is less easily done, but still more doable than surviving as a writer or a painter in an indifferent world. Leading a creative life in the arts and making it pay, while never caving in and betraying your standards, is the hardest course of all.

You can't fake it, although many try. Ruth Bendickson was one who tried, and the shallow meaning it had given her life, even amplified by her great success, must have been clear to her at some level. And now she thought she had defeated me, the one person who could derail her. She had settled for the appearance of being an important writer, and the illusion was buoyed up by the money she made. As a portrait painter, I could see the falseness of it in her face beneath the firm lines of triumph. She may not have known it was there. Gradually, however, she saw something in my face she recognized as her defeat. I lifted the cup to my lips for a moment, then set it back down on the tablecloth without tasting it. Her eyes didn't flicker. We still were frozen in that gaze as Diego Delgado appeared on the run from the left, a gun in his outstretched hand.

From the right, Officer Ignacio Ramos was also speeding toward our table from the far end of the bar. Ruth evidently caught them both in her peripheral vision, but her eyes stayed locked on mine. Her left hand shot out and swept my coffee cup off the table, where it shattered against the top edge of a planter and fell in pieces to the stone floor. She rose, stumbling backwards three feet to the rail, her eyes still fixed on mine, never wavering, until she twisted herself to one side and plunged over the parapet. Her scream lasted but a couple of seconds, when it was abruptly cut off. As brief as it was, the silence

that followed was stunning. I couldn't bring myself to rise and look over the rail to see how Ruth
Bendickson had died.

Delgado stopped ten feet from the edge of
the table, replacing his gun in its shoulder holster. I
wasn't sure what held him off; I hadn't moved. Ramos hung over the parapet, his hands gripping the
iron gallery rail. I felt at once responsible for Ruth's
death, and yet not. Maya had told me Ruth had
speculated that Barlow was the catalyst in Amy
Wendt's suicide, but not the cause of it. "No one
can make you kill yourself," Ruth had told Maya, or
words to that effect. Her own death was waiting for
her in the wings, and it had taken my cue.

"That was close, yes?" asked Delgado, moving once again. Uncharacteristically he placed a
hand my shoulder. "But she chose to die rather than
to pay you."

"Not so close, and it wasn't about the money.
She knew I had her on Barlow's death. Now I don't
think there's enough of the coffee left to test on the
floor, or in that planter." The truth was that lab tests
no longer mattered to me. They were no more than
punctuation on a story already written.

"No." Delgado picked up an emptied packet
of artificial sweetener from the table and pinched

it open so he could look inside. "But I think there's enough residue caught in the creases here for the lab to work with. It's easier when it's not dissolved and mixed with coffee."

EPILOGUE

I would've thought Maya would be the one to mourn Ruth Bendickson the most because she was a fan of her work, but that was not the case. She's offended when people try to kill me, no matter how good they are as writers, or as anything else. And then there was the question of how good Ruth really was as a writer. I guess you'd have to read her only book, the last one of the Rachel trilogy, to know. It's probably selling even better since her death.

Always the realist, Cody thought Ruth got what she deserved. He has no patience with murder, and his old cop instinct suggested that when the guilty kill themselves to avoid trial, they save the justice system and the taxpayer some real money. It's a win-win situation, he said, especially in an era of tight budgets. After all, he added, innocent people don't kill themselves. I didn't comment, thinking of Amy Wendt, a tragic young woman who was only guilty of being unable to handle the world as she found it. There are much greater sins than that, and most of them go unpunished.

It will be no surprise that I found a different level on which to connect with the tragedy of Ruth Bendickson. Repeating to myself that she had faked it, that she had stolen the work of a poor suicide, still left me with sympathy for her great but unrealizable ambition. Perhaps her argument of the imperative of need still held some weight for me too, and after all, Amy had indeed walked away from her life and her work because of the explosive combination of her mental disease and Justus Barlow's mental abuse. This didn't make her books belong to anyone else, but her absence made their theft less heinous. After all, Amy's loss was self-induced. Ruth had only robbed Michael, and to a lesser extent, her readers, by her dishonesty. And in the end, the readers still had the books to read, which many would probably say was an acceptable tradeoff, feeling the content was more important than the author's identity.

So, is honesty required of the artist? Maybe, but it may also be a moving target, too difficult to define. I would go so far as to say with more certainty that the artist ought at least to do his own work. Maya had told me about best selling authors whose name was still on the cover but who hadn't done the writing inside. I guess writing and publishing have become a rather dodgy business, as Ruth suggested. After all, she would know better than most.

And as Ruth herself had told Maya, no one can make you kill yourself. Was the suicide of both her and Amy in some strange way the legacy of the Rachel (Rebecca) books? I made a note to suggest to Michael Wendt that if he filed a claim against Ruth's estate, we'd be happy to furnish materials to support it. It would provide some small justice for him, since those books had been a source of lethal misery in his life.

Because I had taken the brunt of the endgame, Maya and Cody both volunteered to deliver the final Zacher Agency report to Chad Metcalf. I said I'd rather do it myself. They acquiesced, thinking I meant I needed closure, but I was already beyond that. It was not that I thought such a conversation would yield any more resolution for me at all, or that Chad didn't already know the great majority of the events that had finished the case. According to Delgado, the police had contacted and briefed him the same day about the demise of Ruth Bendickson.

I had no better reason to go myself than wanting to see his reaction.

But Chad Metcalf was not easily ambushed, although I imagine many have tried. When I entered his office I could see he was prepared for me, and I wondered whether, in some way, I'd already been spun myself by the Metcalf spin machine. I felt like it, and my knees and elbows still creaked when I got up or sat down.

"There was no need to kill Ruth like that, Zacher," he said as I walked in. This was his greeting. "I realize you didn't actually push her over the parapet, but you might as well have, you know? She could've written more books from prison. That guy who Norman Mailer helped did that, and it was still published. The little people out there eat that kind of thing up. Underdog stuff, I call it. The real problem now is that Ruth didn't even have a chance to give her closing remarks. It's only twenty minutes at the end of the conference when some of the people are already gone, but even so. They pay good money every year to come to this affair, and I feel obliged to give them what they paid for, dammit."

"Sorry," I said. There was nothing I could add that would make any sense to either of us. Chad had no need for an additional report from the Zacher Agency. He knew all the facts; he had spun them for his own purposes and was already moving on.

Mentally, he must have been settling into Maui for next year's meeting. Bob Crais was probably waiting for his call. I glanced at the end of the bar, where, above the short refrigerator and next to the coffee-pot, rested a bronze urn that must have contained the late book doctor's remains. I could just make out, in the ornate style of Gothic lettering I thought of as high school trophy script, the name *Barlow*.

"Now I'm going to have to give those remarks myself," Chad went on, rubbing his hands together, "because there's sure as hell no one else of Ruth's stature here but me. What the hell am I supposed to say?" Inspiration lit his face. "Hey! Could Maya write something for me?"

He appeared to be unaware of the irony in this.

"I don't think so, Chad. The Zacher Agency is moving on to its next case now. Why not simply explain what happened and give your regrets to the conference? Don't spin it, and don't get hold of the PR guy in New York, because he's probably tied up with Sally Field right now. And surely keep Lola under wraps as you do it. Put it out there straight, the way it really was."

I stood up and placed an envelope containing his bill on the desk in front of him. He didn't offer to shake hands, nor did I. He had touched me in other ways that I would not quickly forget, although I might try. As I turned to walk out the door of his office, the blank look on his face defined the way I'll always remember Chad Metcalf.

It was the Friday after the conference ended. The staff had folded their tents and fled the disorder their visit had caused. A murder and a suicide in the same week make for a rare tragedy here. A messenger had come by the house with a check from Chad Metcalf, this time enclosed within an envelope. We were in good shape again, although this time I thought we'd avoid celebrating on the rooftop bar of the Rosewood Hotel.

Maya had gone to *centro* to have lunch with a friend, and when she returned, she slapped the newspaper down on the counter in the kitchen. *Atención* is a weekly, and it comes out on Fridays.

"We've been spun," she said. "Spun right out of existence. It's like we were never there." She opened the paper to page five. There, framed in black, was the following announcement:

MYSTERY WRITERS RESPOND

In response to queries about the fatal events that occurred at the recent San Miguel session of the International Mystery Writers' Conference (IMWC), their New York spokesperson has issued the following statement:

The IMWC deeply regrets the two recent deaths that occurred during this year's conference in México. The internationally known mystery writer, Ruth Bendickson, died of head injuries resulting from a fall to the pavement. While the colonial charm of San Miguel de Allende is widely known, the dark side of that is a maze of nearly medieval cobblestone streets and alleys, as well as narrow, uneven sidewalks that can be a pitfall for anyone who's more accustomed to the smooth, professionally finished walkways of the United States. This was Ruth's undoing. We will miss her indeed.

The other victim at the conference was the well-known editor and literary consultant, Justus Barlow. Mr. Barlow, a legend in the publishing business, had the misfortune to mistakenly overdose on his own heart medication, with fatal effects. He died peacefully, in his sleep.

Ironically, it was in the early days of his consulting business when Ruth Bendickson approached Justus Barlow with her great best seller, *Rachel's Folly*, still in manuscript, that she received the astute counsel that led to its publication and immediate success. Now they have both left us.

The Director of the Conference, Mr. Chad Metcalf, has asked me to add that next year's conference, in Maui, will be dedicated to the memory of these two great individuals, whose contribution to the world of letters can never be overstated.

Please visit the author's website@

www.sanmiguelallendebooks.com

JOHN SCHERBER

www.ingramcontent.com/pod-product-compliance
Lightning Source LLC
Chambersburg PA
CBHW030956260626
47169CB00002B/568